Everything is a Game of Beliefs

Also by Sirshree

* Spiritual Masterpieces- Self Realisation books for serious seekers *

The Secret of Awakening
Secret of the Third Side of the Coin : Unravelling Missing Links in Spirituality
100% Karma : Learn the Art of Conscious Karma that Liberates
100% Wisdom : Wisdom that leads you to experience and be established in your true nature
You are Meditation : Discover Peace and Bliss Within
Essence of Devotion : From Devotee to Divinity
Dip into Oneness : Beyond Knower, Known and Knowing
The Unshaken Mind : Discovering the Purpose, Power and Potential of your mind
The Supreme Quest : Your search for the Truth ends there where you are
The Greatest Freedom : Discover the key to an Awakened Living
Seek Forfiveness & be Free : Liberation from Karmic Bondage
Passwords to a Happy Life : The Art of Being Happy in all Situaltion
The Light of Grace : Why Guru, God, Grace and You are one
Why Jesus Didn't Work A Miracle During Crucifixion
Secrets of Shiva

* Self Help Treasures - Self Development books for success seekers *

The Source of Health: The Key to Perfect Health Discovery
Inner Ninety Hidden Infinity : How to build your book of values
Inner 90 for Youth : The secret of reaching and staying at the peak of success
The Source for Youth : You have the power to change your life
Inner Magic : The Power of self-talk
The Five Supreme Secrets of Life : Unveiling the Ways to Attain Wealth, Love and God
Freedom from Failure : 7 Spiritual Secrets that Transform Failure into a Blessing
You are Not Lazy : A story of shifting from Laziness to Success
Freedom From Fear, Worry, Anger : How to be cool, calm and courageous
Mastering the Art of Decision Making : How to Make the Highest Choice
Complete Parenting : How to raise your child with grace

* New Age Nuggets - Practical books on applied spirituality and self help *

The Source : Power of Happy Thoughts
Secret of Happiness : Instant Happiness - Here and Now!
Excuse me God... : Fulfilling your wishes through the Power of Prayer and Seed of Faith
Help God to Help You : Whatever you do, do it with a smile
Ultimate Purpose of Success: Achieving Success in all five aspects of life
Celebrating Relationships : Bringing Love, Life, Laughter in Your Relations
Everything is a Game of Beliefs : Understanding is the Whole Thing
Detachment From Attachment : Gift of Freedom From Suffering
Emotional Freedom Through Spiritual Wisdom
The Miracle Mind : How to master your mind before it masters you
The Power of Present : Experience the Joy of the Now

* Profound Parables - Fiction books containing profound truths *

Beyond Life : Conversations on Life After Death
The Source @ Work : A Story of Inspiration from Jeeodee
The One Above : What if God was your neighbour?
The Warrior's Mirror : The Path To Peace
Master of Siddhartha: Revealing the Truth of Life and After-life
Put Stress to Rest : Utilizing Stress to Make Progress

Everything is a Game of Beliefs

Understanding is the whole thing

SIRSHREE

Everything is a game of beliefs
By **Sirshree** Tejparkhi

Copyright © Tejgyan Global Foundation
All Rights Reserved 2019

Tejgyan Global Foundation is a charitable organization with its headquarters in Pune, India.

ISBN : 978-81-84154-10-8

Published by WOW Publishings Pvt. Ltd., India

First edition published in July 2014

Third edition published in June 2017

First reprint in December 2019

Copyrights are reserved with Tejgyan Global Foundation and publishing rights are vested exclusively with WOW Publishings Pvt. Ltd. This book is sold subject to the condition that it shall not by way of trade or otherwise, be lent, resold, hired out, or otherwise circulated without the publisher's prior written consent in any form of binding or cover other than that in which it is published and without a similar condition including this condition being imposed on the subsequent purchaser and without limiting the rights under copyright reserved above, no part of this publication may be reproduced, stored in or introduced into a retrieval system, or transmitted, in any form, or by any means, electronic, mechanical, photocopying, recording or otherwise, without the prior written permission of both the copyright owner and the above-mentioned publisher of this book. Any person who does any unauthorized act in relation to this publication may be liable to criminal prosecution and civil claims for damages.

Although the author and publisher have made every effort to ensure accuracy of content in this book, they hereby disclaim any liability to any party for any loss, damage, or disruption caused by errors or omissions, resulting from negligence, accident, or any other cause. Readers are advised to take full responsibility to exercise discretion in understanding and applying the content of this book.

*To our forefathers who took the
support of belief systems,
so as to make us alert and aware
while treading the journey of life.*

Table Of Contents

Preface	9
How to read this book	12
SECTION I - Demystifying Beliefs	13
1. Beliefs and their origin	15
2. A Tree of Beliefs	19
SECTION II - Demystifying Success	23
3. Myths about Success	25
4. Myths about Money	31
5. Myths about Time	40
6. Myths about Confidence	46
SECTION III - Demystifying Relationships	61
7. Myths about Love	63
8. Myths about Marriage	69
9. Myths about Parenting	73
SECTION IV - Demystifying Death	81
10. Myths about Death and related Rites and Rituals	83

SECTION V - Demystifying Divinity		93
11.	Myths about God	95
12.	General Myths about Spirituality	105
13.	Myths about Prayer	119
14.	Myths about Meditation	127
15.	Some Myths about the Guru	137
16.	Myths about Self-realization	142

SECTION VI - Demystifying Superstitions		171
17.	An urban survey on superstitions	173
18.	Superstitions related to Luck	175
19.	Superstitions related to People and their Behaviour	178
20.	Superstitions related to Eating Habits	183
21.	Superstitions related to Fights	187
22.	Superstitions related to Days and Dates	191
23.	Superstitions related to Household Articles	194
24.	Superstitions related to Business	199
25.	Superstitions related to Babies and Pregnant Women	202
26.	Superstitions related to Animals	207
	Appendices	211

Preface

From our childhood we all, without exception, take in a myriad of beliefs. We get these beliefs from our parents, family, and friends, as well as from our environment. Certain core beliefs have been directly handed over to us. Others we have acquired by observing our surroundings.

Some of these beliefs were required for our safety and mental security while we were young. These were presented in a simple manner to ensure a child's mind would understand. As we grew up and began to develop a better understanding of life we no longer needed those beliefs. Many of us, however, continue to live in the prison of those limiting beliefs. We blindly follow them without ever questioning their validity.

Some examples of beliefs are: "So much to do, but so little time"; "People who have more money are better than me"; "I can't be successful without good English speaking skills"; "Love diminishes with time"; "A couple's horoscopes should be matched for a successful marriage"; "After someone dies, the surviving family members are required to perform rituals related to death"; "One should bow to the deity in a temple, otherwise it will become angry"; "A special time, place, and environment are essential in order to offer a meaningful prayer"; "The number 13 is unlucky"; "If a cat crosses your path, it's bad luck". We're sure you can add many more to this list.

When we understand the truth behind these beliefs, then we finally realize that we aren't required to abide by them. However, a vast majority of us still unquestioningly hold onto beliefs like these, which only causes us to lead a constricted and limited life. In fact, when we gain an understanding of the truth, we realize that these beliefs are the root of many of the stresses and burdens we carry with us. They're the real culprits behind all sorrow.

The time has come to get into the very depths of these beliefs and understand the reality behind them. Gaining this understanding allows us to be liberated from them once and for all. As we start seeing the world as it really is, without the distorting filters of beliefs, we open ourselves to the experience of love and joy in our lives.

This book is a conclusive myth-buster. It will help you to understand and reassess everything related to your set of beliefs. As you read, keep in mind the words "belief" and "myth" are used interchangeably.

The book is divided into six sections:

Section I: "Demystifying Beliefs"— throws light on the crux of beliefs and their origins. It explains the tree of beliefs.

Section II: "Demystifying Success"— unearths myths about time, money, confidence and success.

Section III: "Demystifying Relationships"— addresses myths about love, marriage and parenting.

Section IV: "Demystifying Death"— explains myths about death and rebirth, as well as its associated rites and rituals.

Section V: "Demystifying Divinity"— expounds on myths about God, spirituality, prayer, meditation, Guru, and Self-realization.

Section VI: "Demystifying Superstitions"— explains various superstitions and the truth behind them.

After providing a general understanding about what beliefs really are, their origin, and the tree of beliefs in Section I, the following sections explain individual myths. Each myth is followed by "Reality", an explanation of the truth behind it. Many myths are also followed by a "Revelation", another look at applying these truths to our lives. As you go through the book you will come to truly understand reality. Everything is a game of beliefs; understanding is everything.

Enjoy reading this book and being liberated from the prison of beliefs in the process. Best wishes as you embark on the journey toward freedom!

How to read this book

This book is divided into six sections. Each section has a variety of myths categorized into separate chapters.

You can read this book cover to cover, or you may begin by reading the section that interests you the most.

1. If you want to know what beliefs are, how they have originated, and their structure, you may read Section I: Demystifying Beliefs.

2. Section II: Demystifying Success will help you understand roadblocks in attaining success, managing your time, confidence building, andmoney management.

3. You can blossom in your relationships after having read Section III: Demystifying Relationships. This section throws light on myths related to love, marriage and parenting.

4. If you are curious to know about death, reasons behind the rituals followed after death, and rebirth, consider reading Section IV: Demystifying Death.

5. If you want to gain clarity about the myths related to God, spirituality, prayer, meditation, Guru, and Self-realization, Section V: Demystifying Divinity will be of help to you.

6. Whether you believe in any superstitions or not, Section VI: Demystifying Superstitions will throw more clarity on this topic. This section covers superstitions related to a variety of categories such as luck, people and their behavior, eating habits, fights, days and dates, household articles, business, babies and pregnant women, and animals.

7. References made to temples can be considered to mean any holy place.

SECTION I

Demystifying Beliefs

1
Beliefs and their origin

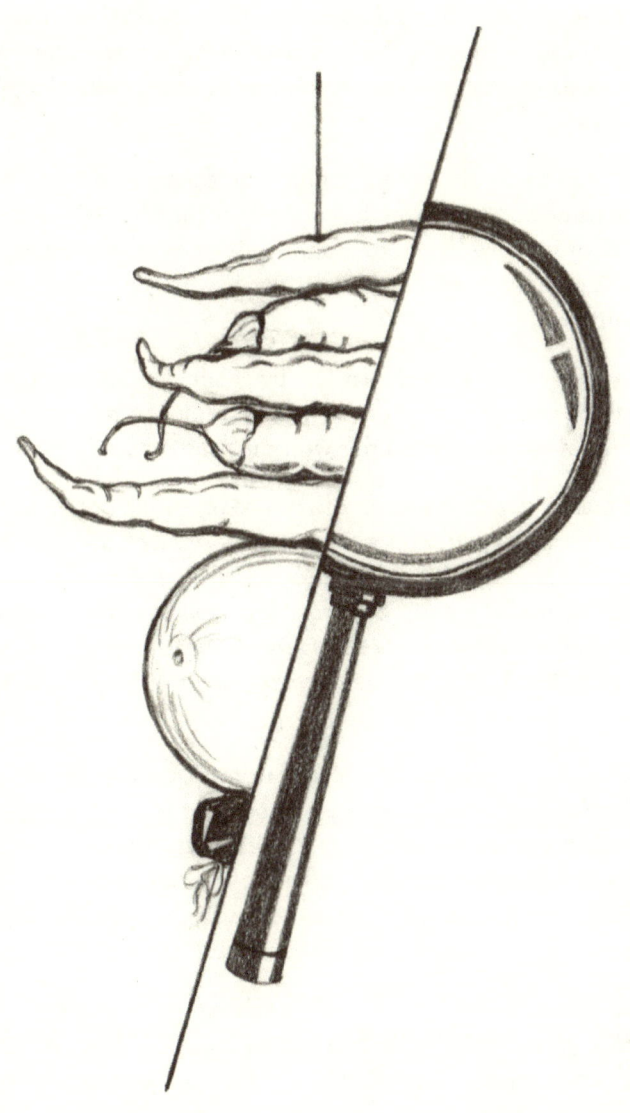

In this chapter we'll understand what beliefs are and how they originate. Most people trust their own views of life, and believe that whatever they have assumed about life is true. When they are not able to handle certain challenges, they justify themselves by blaming external factors for their failures. However, when things are explained to them from a completely new perspective the truth of life dawns upon them.

After sincere and deceit-free contemplation, they understand that the actual cause of their failures does not lie in the external environment, but rather in the numerous beliefs that entrap them. Whatever they wanted in life was available from the very beginning, but their beliefs stopped them from seeing it.

In fact, after in-depth contemplation, one comes to see that beliefs are the root cause of all suffering in life, be it at the physical, mental, social, financial, or spiritual level. So, if one wants to excel in all areas of life, he needs to first understand what beliefs are, how they originate, and how to get rid of them.

You may be amazed to hear that just by gaining an understanding about your beliefs, you can get rid of them easily. How can it be so simple!? But indeed it is! Let's understand this with the help of an example:

An alcoholic is standing outside a garden holding onto the fence. He moves around the garden and shouts, "Get me out of here!" He does not realize that he is already outside. If someone were to tell him that he is already free, then he would get angry. A sensible person wouldn't contradict him. The sensible person would take him around the garden, and in the process would turn him in the opposite direction, saying, "Now you are free. You can go."

Understanding your beliefs has a similar impact. Knowing the truth will not only change the direction of your course in life, but will also liberate you from constricting beliefs. Therefore, it is said, "Everything is a game of beliefs. Understanding is the whole thing." Understanding is complete in itself. Here is an example that will make it easier to understand how beliefs impact the way you perceive events and circumstances:

Four people were looking at a child, and each one was asked, "What do you think of this child?" The first person said, "He looks dreadful." The second person replied, "He is delicate." The third person responded, "He is okay." The fourth person exclaimed, "He is the most beautiful baby I have ever seen!"

How was the child in reality? No one could explain that completely, as their opinions were based on their beliefs. The beliefs an Indian person will hold regarding eyes, hair, and skin complexion will vary from those of an African, Chinese, or American person. If a skin specialist looks at the child, he will look at his skin. However, if an eye specialist looks at the child, his focus will be on his eyes. We can see that beliefs vary from one person to another, one family to another, one profession to another, one religion to another, one country to another, and so on. Therefore, it is said that beauty is in the eye of the beholder; that is, in the beliefs that look out from the eye of the beholder.

Whenever we see anything, the truth of the matter is that we always add something to it based on our beliefs. Because of this habit we can't see anything as it truly is. In order to excel in all areas of life, it is required to get rid of preconceived notions and assumptions.

When we think in terms of labels—when we believe we must pronounce judgments on all things—then those labels naturally give birth to thoughts of "good" or "bad". That's when the cycle of happiness and unhappiness begins. When we understand the game of beliefs, we stop labeling issues as "good" or "bad"; we are able to see everything as it is without any labels.

When we're presented with an event or a circumstance, we receive evidence for whatever we believe. If we believe people are not good, we will inevitably meet people who reinforce that belief. Our beliefs impact others, just as the beliefs of others impact us. In fact, our beliefs transmit a message to the subconscious mind of all the people around us.

Now we can see how the game of beliefs has been going on in the background, and we didn't have the slightest clue about its existence. Simply by gaining an understanding of the game of beliefs we learn to break free from its maze. A life free of beliefs is a life full of happiness and bliss. Who would not want to have such a life!?

One might wonder how these beliefs came into existence in the first place. Again, this is easily understood with the help of another example.

There was once a priest who prayed daily. He had a cat which was very playful. Whenever he would sit for his prayers, she would come and disturb him. She would meddle with his prayer plate, extinguish the lamp, and tear apart the garland. He was troubled by all this. He tried leaving the cat outside the house and closing the door, but the cat would then scratch and knock at the door with her paws. So, he brought the cat inside the house, but tied her so that she could come near the prayer area but could not put her paws in the prayer plate. Thus, the problem was solved and the priest could continue with his prayers. The priest developed a following, and they watched as he conducted the prayers in this particular way.

One day the priest died. The disciples, wanting to continue the rituals of their Master, started the prayer practice. Then they remembered that the priest used to tie a cat before he started each prayer. They searched for the cat, but she was nowhere to be found; so they found a random cat instead. After that, it became a ritual to tie a cat before each prayer practice.

We can understand that the actual reason for tying the cat had nothing to do with the ritual, but it was adopted out of blind faith. Even today, many practices are being followed blindly which simply aren't necessary. Someone initiated a certain action in response to a specific, unique circumstance at a certain time. Eventually this action came to be followed unquestioningly, although its original reason had long since passed. There are a plethora of such beliefs ingrained in today's society. If one wants to get rid of one's beliefs, one needs to understand them in detail.

The next chapter deals with different types of beliefs, so that all unnecessary beliefs can be eliminated step by step.

■ ■ ■

2
A Tree of Beliefs

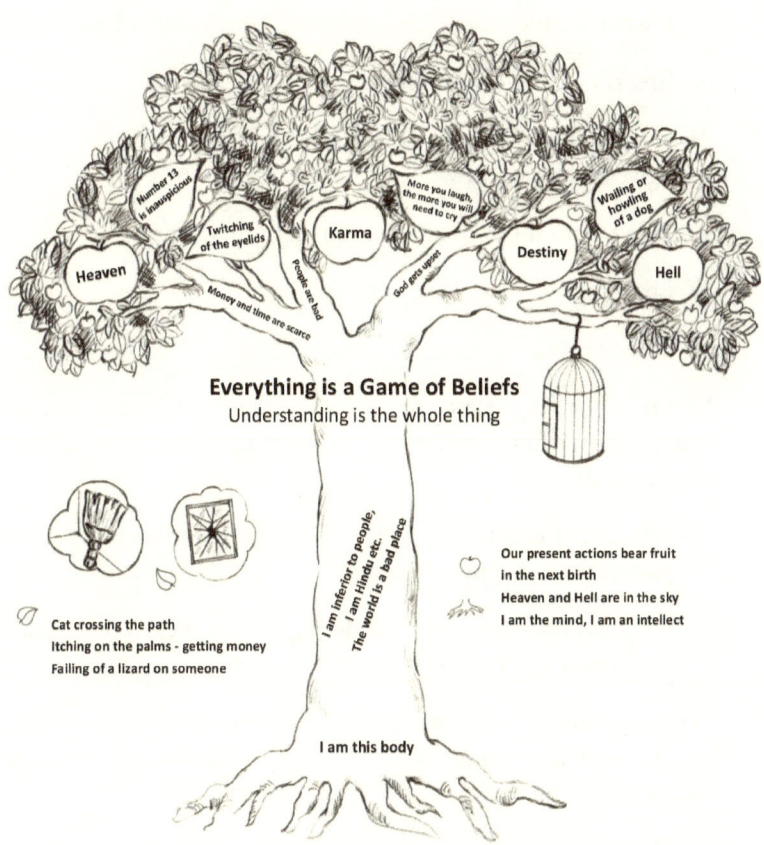

We can more fully understand different types of beliefs by comparing them to the various parts of a tree.

Some beliefs are as superficial and easily-discarded as the leaves or flowers of a tree. More central beliefs, those having to do with our actions and their consequences, are "fruit" beliefs, which require a deeper understanding to transcend. Some beliefs are stronger still, like branches or a trunk, and require understanding, contemplation, and implementation together. Root beliefs are so fundamentally ingrained that one does not ever stop to re-examine them.

1. **"Leaf beliefs"** are outer or superficial beliefs. Examples:

    a. If a black cat crosses your path something bad will happen.

    b. Breaking a mirror brings bad luck.

2. **"Flower beliefs"** are also superficial, but sound appealing because they give an illusion of wisdom. Examples:

    a. Don't shower too much love upon your children.

    b. Love is blind.

    c. Money is evil.

3. **"Fruit beliefs"** are related to action and the fruits (consequences) of action. They include beliefs related to karma, destiny, hell, heaven, etc. Examples:

    a. Whatever suffering you endure in your present life is the result of your actions in a previous life.

    b. If person has performed bad deeds then he goes to hell; if he has performed good deeds, he goes to heaven.

4. **"Branch beliefs"** are assumptions about yourself or about society which you have taken on unquestioningly. Like a strong branch, they require much more time to be felled. Examples:

    a. Time and money are both limited.

    b. You must compromise your personal values to become successful.

    c. I have a poor personality because I don't look good, or I don't look smart.

5. **"Trunk beliefs"** are very strongly held beliefs. They seem helpful, even required, for living in society. However, even they should be dropped, lest they become a cause for bondage. Some examples of "trunk" beliefs are:

    a. I am a Muslim, or a Hindu, or a Christian, or a Sikh, or a Parsi, or a Jain.

    b. I am superior or inferior to others.

6. **If "trunk"** beliefs are very strongly held beliefs about society and your place in it, then "root" beliefs have to do with your very own identity. Even though it may seem that your very life depends on them, it is important that even these beliefs be transcended. Examples:

    a. I am the body.

    b. I am the mind.

    c. I am the intellect.

All these different types of beliefs are explained in detail in the forthcoming sections of this book.

■ ■ ■

SECTION II

Demystifying Success

3
Myths about Success

Y ou probably are one of the many individuals who are working hard; hoping success will somehow bless you. At the same time, you may also be a bit skeptical that it ever will. If you're like many, you may be clinging to basic success myths. These mistaken beliefs may actually limit your ability to attain the success you desperately seek.

 **Myths**

1. Without knowledge, you can't be successful.
2. Without education, you won't be successful.
3. Without English skills, you can't be successful.
4. Without luck, you can't be successful.
5. Without good references and contacts, you will never be successful.
6. Without a woman behind you, you can't be successful.
7. You need to have been born into a wealthy family to be successful.

 **Reality**

Though each of the above components could be helpful in attaining success, regardless of the area in which you're working, none of them is guaranteed to help you achieve your goals and dreams. Look around you. There are plenty of individuals attaining their goals who don't fit into any of the categories above. The reality is your success doesn't depend on any of these factors.

Revelation

In order to achieve true and lasting success, you only need to take three actions. Follow this "success achievement triad" and your success is practically guaranteed. These three actions can be easily described by the saying "On your mark, get set, and go."

a. Decide your aim (On your mark…)
b. Prepare for your aim (Get set…)
c. Plan your work and work your plan (Go.)

 **Myths**

8. It takes a lot . of time to be successful.

9. Success comes only with experience.

10. Success means a lot of work.

 **Reality**

These may be three of the largest myths concerning success which people believe. They are really nothing more than false impressions of how others supposedly have achieved success.

We can quickly dispel these. First, it doesn't necessarily take a great deal of time to be successful. Many individuals experience success through innovation fairly quickly and easily. Secondly, people have become successful regardless of their age. If others can do it, you too can certainly do it.

Finally, success doesn't always mean you have to invest a tremendous amount of work in order to experience it. Sometimes opportunity beckons in the strangest of ways. It stands before us in various guises. That's exactly what makes success seem elusive and even discriminatory to some of us.

 Revelation

Every problem and every difficulty is actually an opportunity disguised in the garb of unhappiness. The old saying is true: "Opportunity knocks." What you may not know, though, is that most of the time opportunity knocks at the back door. Many of us fail to answer it, or worse yet, we may even deny its entry. That's why you must be aware of every opportunity that knocks at your door.

 **Myths**

11. You need to know the business to become successful.

12. You need capital to become successful. Everything boils down to money.

13. You will only find success if you have something unique and innovative.

 **Reality**

There are plenty of examples of successful people who had little or no money or lacked knowledge; yet despite this, they achieved great success. How did they do it? They relied on their ability to inspire others. If you don't believe you have the power to inspire, just look around. You're constantly learning from those who have inspired others to serve the vision they would like to accomplish. They inspire with knowledge, with capital, with management skills, and with innovation.

Revelation

One of the simplest, yet most powerful, methods of inspiration is through the application of the golden rule: "Do unto others what you want others to do unto you." Follow this rule and you will be amazed at how successful you can be. In other words, your actions can be just as inspiring — if not more so — than anything you can say to someone.

 **Myths**

14. In order to become successful, you must make sacrifices.

15. You must compromise your personal life to become successful.

16. You must compromise your personal values to become successful.

17. You have to give up your principles and stop being honest to be successful.

18. When you are successful, you will have more enemies than friends.

19. You cannot always be successful. Those individuals who experience the good in life in the form of success are sure to experience the bad in the form of failures after a time.

20. You will not be able to sleep at night when you become successful.

 **Reality**

It really is possible to be successful and honest at the same time. In fact, it can be said that honesty is an essential ingredient for success. It is also possible to attain success while maintaining a healthy balance between work and personal life. Indeed, it is also possible to experience success on a consistent basis. Look around to see the number of individuals and companies who are doing just this.

Revelation

In order to achieve a balance between your work and your personal life, you must first learn to master the art of completion. This is exactly what it sounds like. All you need to do is complete everything you start. Unless you develop this ability, you won't be able to achieve equilibrium between your work and your personal life.

Consider this question for a moment: Are you repeatedly distracted with thoughts of the past or the future?

Do you know why? It's because the present moment is incomplete. Why would a person be disturbed by dreams at night? It's because many of his tasks are left incomplete during the day, and his subconscious mind completes them through dreaming. To avoid this, you simply need to complete everything and become "complete with everyone".

Even your relationships can be incomplete. "Completing with people" means you tell people what you feel. If you are annoyed with someone, you "complete with them" by saying, "I am annoyed because of what you did." Take notice of this very simple approach for handling your relationships.

You probably have already recognized that this is not how most people deal with others. Instead of entering into a calm discussion, they place actions at either end of a spectrum. At one end, they'll say, "You idiot, why did you do that?" At the other, they'll remain silent about an incident. Neither approach is good. Even though it may be the more difficult route, in the long run it is much better to follow the middle path. Complete with the other person by sharing exactly what you feel instead of trying to prove him wrong. Try this. You will discover how liberating it really is.

■ ■ ■

4
Myths about Money

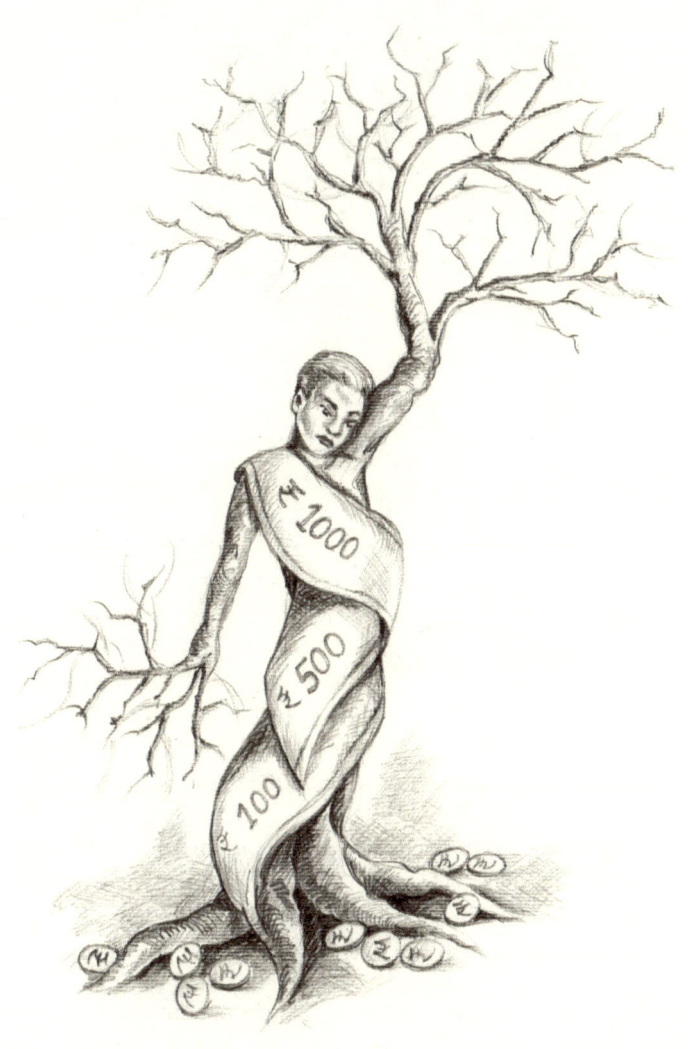

It's time to turn our attention to some commonly held myths about money. The English language is rich with phrases which subtly — even perhaps subliminally — teach us that "money is the root of all evil." For example, how many times have you said, "He was filthy rich"?

Many families, either knowingly or on an unconscious level, teach their children to believe that all businessmen are dishonest, or unethical, or both.

Some even teach their children that it's wrong to borrow money. Others are led to believe that having big financial dreams is mere foolishness. After all, the argument goes, there's only so much money to go around. It's a scarce commodity.

Are you surprised to discover that the children who are told these things are so steeped in poor money values that becoming rich is not even a viable option for them?

Unfortunately, they carry these myths into adulthood. Let's look at just a few of these mental money blockages and "negative money messages".

 Myths

1. Money is everything.
2. Money is God.
3. Money is power.
4. Money is the only thing that counts.
5. Life is not worth living without money.
6. Without money, I am nothing.
7. Without money, I will perish.
8. I should worship those who have money.
9. Money will buy me everyone's love.
10. People who have money are better than me.

 **Reality**

Let's clear up the deep-seated myth that is behind all the above myths right now: money in and of itself doesn't hold any power. None! It's nothing but a medium of exchange. The power lies in people, not in money. Don't ever attribute your power to a dead object such as money.

Then the question arises: what is money? If money is not power, then what is it exactly? It's just one of the many tools used to express and transfer power — nothing more! There are thousands who do not have money, but they are still able to live wonderful lives based on the relationships they have nurtured.

Revelation

Considering money to be of no value at all or believing it to be everything are two polarities of the spectrum. Keep in mind, money does not have any value other than what you ascribe to it.

Myths

11. I should stay away from money.

12. I should dislike and not trust people who have money. They're selfish, corrupt, unethical, and dishonest.

13. Money is bad.

14. Money is the root cause of all evil.

15. Money begets misery.

Reality

Money is neither good nor bad in and of itself. It is merely a medium of exchange. The ill effects attributed to the inherent bad reputation of money are not justified; they really originate in your mind. Depending on your perspective, you project a positive or negative reputation onto wealth. Don't attribute the wrong doings of man to "money".

Revelation

Money is neither a demon nor God. Neither spend it superfluously nor spend it stingily. Neither run away from it nor get stuck with it. Money is money; use it, and forget about it until your next need arises. Earn money and reach your destination by turning it into a path. Money is not the end destination; it is merely a means to the end.

Myths

16. The more the money you have, the less you grow spiritually.

17. More money inevitably leads to poor relationships.

Reality

The truth is that somebody who has not educated himself in how to handle the world around him blames his failure on something outside of himself. He can't succeed. He'll endlessly explain that his failure is due to money (usually a lack of it), or time (again usually a lack of it), or poor relationships. It is not his fault. If this sounds like you, you're likely protesting that it's not your fault either.

Your success in life is determined by how you have trained yourself and have grown as an individual, be it in relationships, time, or spirituality. If you lack this training you may commit a host of mistakes unknowingly. You may even find yourself incapable of managing your friends and relatives. The root cause of this is not necessarily the lack or abundance of money. What is needed is a proper education and training in its use.

When you grow spiritually, you automatically begin to learn to use money in a whole new fashion. You will discover a respect for it that you never had before. *Instead of blocking the flow of money in your life, this newfound detachment helps — perhaps for the first time — to attract more into your life. Instead of thinking of yourself as a slave to money, you become a master of currency.*

Revelation

Remember: there are many people who have lots of money and also have great relationships. There are many who have money and are spiritually growing at the same time. If it is possible for them, it is possible for you too. More money does not mean less spirituality or less relationships. More money simply means one thing: "more money".

Myths

18. Only the educated can become rich.

19. Those in the working class cannot be rich. Only the business class can become rich.

20. I cannot manage money. Handling money is difficult.

Reality

What do all these myths have in common? They all approach money from a negative perspective, and affirm feelings that you're unable to do certain actions. The truth is that you have the power to manage all the money in the world. Many individuals are uneducated but are rich. There are many who are performing routine jobs and yet are rich. If it is possible for them, it is possible for you, too.

Revelation

Here is a truth that you may not have known, and it may surprise you: There is plenty of money for everyone. All that is needed is "one creative idea". There is no money problem. There is only an idea problem. The real issue is that people drain their creative energy chasing money all their lives. Always remember that new ideas help you create whatever you want.

Myths

21. Earning money requires hard work.

22. Money is hard to come by.

23. No matter how hard we work, we'll always be poor.

Reality

The art of attracting money requires you to work smarter, not necessarily harder. When you keep repeating that attaining money is difficult, it becomes difficult. Instead, tell yourself that money comes to you smoothly and easily. In effect, you will attract money much in the same way a magnet attracts metal. Making money is only as difficult as you believe it to be.

Never go after easy money through illegal methods. There is no need to steal, embezzle or misrepresent yourself in the process of creating your abundance.

Revelation

Thinking that earning money is difficult or requires a lot of hard work is a mindset that cuts you off from your real power. It is deficit thinking. Approaching the perceived problem from a perspective of lack and scarcity will only backfire and bring you what you worry about.

 **Myths**

24. The rich are bad or selfish.

25. All businessmen are dishonest or unethical.

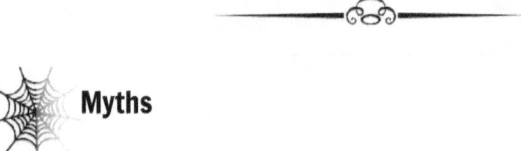 **Reality**

People are people. They are good or bad regardless of whether they are rich or poor. The mere fact that they have money doesn't inherently make them bad individuals

Revelation

Don't fall into the trap that many people do when it comes to thoughts of money. They envy the rich and the successful. When you do this you are sending a message to your mind that you do not want to be like them — that is, you do not want to be rich. In a very real sense you're blocking the prosperity and the flow of abundance that is rightly yours. The saddest part of this is that it's all happening because of erroneous thinking.

 **Myths**

26. When your palm itches, it means that you are going to receive money.

Reality

We do almost all of our work with our hands, so earning money is related to the hands. When you're not working, your hands are idle. That causes pain or discomfort, which is described as itching. This feeling gives an indication for the hands to return to work, which will lead to the acquisition of money. That is how this belief originated.

■ ■ ■

5
Muths about Time

There never seems to be enough time in the day to do everything you want. If you divide your time among your work duties, life with your family, and time by yourself, then you know how true this can be.

 **Myths**

1. There is no time.
2. "So much to do, so little time!"
3. I am poor in managing my time.

 **Reality**

Time is a standard constraint placed on all of us. No single individual receives any more than 24 hours in a day, seven days a week. Some of us, however, would like to have more time. At the very least, we'd like to be more productive with the time we have.

The key is in how we use the time we've been given. We can use it wisely, or we can waste it. There are people in the world who can run companies by spending only 4 hours a week. The great scientist Thomas Alva Edison could utilize his time so effectively that he held a world record of 1,093 patents for a host of inventions and innovations. So, there is no such thing as having no time. The issue is not the amount of time you've been given; it's about how you use that time.

 Revelation

Time management is all about prioritizing what you will be doing and focusing on doing it by eliminating distractions. If we attempt to accomplish too many things at the same time, then we end up completing only a few of them. When the rest of the tasks remain unfinished we get the feeling that there is no time to finish them. Furthermore, we come to believe that we are poor at time management. However, the real problem is not time management, but prioritization.

Furthermore, we lack the relevant skills for certain tasks, and a result we take longer to complete them. Before committing to completion of any task you need to ensure that you're wellequipped with the necessary skills.

 **Myths**

4. Those who are continuously busy are good at time management.
5. Only those who complete tasks at the last moment are truly committed.
6. I am productive only if I work all day long.

 **Reality**

Those who are continuously busy and work until the last moment are actually poor at time management. Successful time management is not about racing the clock and finishing an assignment minutes before the deadline. It's really quite the opposite. It's about effectively completing the target goal on time. In some instances, this could mean before the deadline, depending on the other goals you have and their deadlines.

Revelation

You need to prioritize your most urgent and important tasks. Then, you must plan your other activities accordingly. If you are able to avoid distractions and focus on the goal then you can complete your work on time. However, if you find yourself continuously busy until the last minute, you are likely wasting your time and energy on something other than the identified work.

There are many who thrive in a crisis, and even claim to perform their best work under the pressure of an impending deadline. They delay starting a project, or worse yet, try to improvise until right before the impending deadline.

They create anxiety, not only for themselves, but for others as well. Waiting to start work until the last minute doesn't prove that you're truly committed. On the contrary, the only thing it really proves is that you're not good at managing your time. Had you completed your work according to a plan you wouldn't have needed to burn the midnight oil finishing the project at the last possible moment. In fact, sticking to a plan and completing the work ahead of schedule proves that you are committed. And of course, a wisely set plan also takes into account the need to manage and mitigate risks.

Productivity is not about how many hours you work; it's about how you organize your workload. Some people mistakenly equate being busy with being productive. Do you realize that, generally speaking, only 20 percent of what you do each day produces 80 percent of your results? This is known as the Pareto Principle. The lesson to be learned here is to identify and tackle that productive 20 percent of your activity first. Eliminate the things that don't matter during the workday — they have a minimal effect on your overall productivity. Focus on one task at a time, work on the most important tasks first, and complete them before working on others. You may be surprised to discover that you don't even need to attempt to be productive whole day.

Myths

7. I can get it all done.
8. If I work hard I can complete everything myself.

Reality

These are the biggest myths in time management. Some people feel compelled to do everything on their own. As a result, their to-do list grows day by day. They keep telling themselves that one day they will get up in the morning, and poof! They will get everything done. However, each day has only 24 hours, and no human being can work without sustenance and rest. In fact, there isn't enough time to do it all. So some tasks are always going to be incomplete, especially if we feel the need to do them on our own. Many people, learning these two principles — we can't do it all, and we can't do it all without help — become depressed about their potential success. But when they anticipate being able to complete, or let go of some of their plans, it really comes as a huge relief. It's all right, even natural, if some intended tasks are not completed.

This mindset makes it easier for us to ignore some tasks and desires, as well as delegate some of our tasks to others. Understanding that you will never get all things done helps you make conscious and explicit choices. Instead of letting things haphazardly fall through the cracks, you can intentionally push unimportant things aside and focus your energy on what matters the most.

Revelation

It's more important to do the right thing than to just do right things. In other words, targeted effectiveness is more important than quantity. To determine the "right thing", we need to make deliberate choices that will move us toward the outcomes we most want. Of course, the other side of this scenario is that we need to make deliberate choices about what not to do. Once you prioritize the right things, then you have to "do" them. Learn how to prioritize properly, delegate deliberately, and focus completely.

 Myths

9. Maintaining a "to-do" list, or having the right organizational gadget, will solve my time management problems.
10. I will be good at time management when I find the right system.

 **Reality**

The person around whom the system is built is what ultimately matters, not the system itself. Untold numbers of people maintain a to-do list, and untold numbers of people abandon it after a few days. Having the *fanciest "getting-things-done" app downloaded on your cell phone won't guarantee success.*

Revelation

The "right system" is the one that works for you personally. Continually make small improvements to a productivity system that works for you, and don't give up.

Here are some tips to aid in creating a good time management system for your purposes. Start somewhere — anywhere, in fact — and then customize the system to suit your needs, improving it step by step.

a. At minimum, write down your most important goal-related tasks (or record them in some other fashion). Listing a few areas of focus or goals and grouping tasks within them is a helpful structure.

b. Have a system that allows you to externally capture your thoughts, desires, and ideas, so that you are not carrying them in your head. A small notepad in your pocket or purse will do. Later, you can transfer them to a time management journal or onto your computer.

c. Whatever your system may be, include a way to prioritize.

d. Schedule important appointments and meetings on a calendar. There is no need to schedule your calendar to be 100 percent full. Consult your calendar before you commit yourself to meeting with someone. Be sure you schedule slots for yourself on the calendar as well. Keep these appointments just as you would keep an appointment with an important client — you are that important client.

e. Use technology to help keep your tasks and goals in sync.

f. Review your system weekly, if not daily. This is the most important principle you can practice. Constantly refine and improve your system.

6
Myths about Confidence

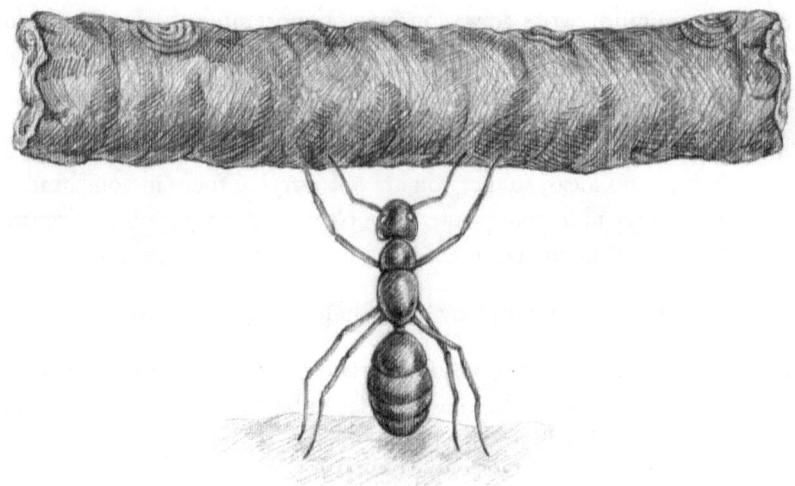

Many people believe that your personality has to do with your physical looks. In truth, your personality and confidence are interlinked. The more we clearly understand the true meaning of personality, the greater our confidence grows. In order to do that, it is important to dispel myths about personality.

 **Myths**

1. I have a poor personality because I don't look good, or I don't look smart.
2. I have a poor personality because I am not rich.
3. I have a poor personality because I am not a good communicator.
4. I have a poor personality because I am not educated.

 **Reality**

There are innumerable examples of those who have not been gifted with outward beauty, yet have powerful, magnetic personalities. Consider some of the most persuasive individuals throughout history: Mahatma Gandhi, Abraham Lincoln, and Mother Teresa, to name a few. Their personalities were strong and compelling, mainly because of the immense faith they possessed.

Similarly, there are countless sports personalities who are neither tall nor handsome, yet they have great personalities. The same is true with a number of character actors and businessmen. They may be too thin or too stout, or they may be bald... yet they are Oscar Award winners or Best Business Personality Award winners. All of these individuals are gifted with talent. Their personalities are not in the least dependent on their physical appearances.

In the same way, your education or bank balance has nothing to do with your personality. Consider the many social workers who are penniless but possess powerful, charismatic personalities. They render a valuable service to society, despite the fact that they do not have bulging wallets or large stacks of money.

Countless numbers of people could be cited here who don't excel in educational achievement but possess powerful, compelling personalities.

Interestingly, personality also does not depend on how good a communicator you are, nor is it dependent on the knowledge you possess. You can probably think of many people who are outstanding public speakers but lack good personalities. It's not the force of their personalities that makes them persuasive public speakers, but rather their knowledge. You may have had the experience of listening to a speaker and being inspired by their words, but when you finally meet them you feel disappointed. You don't feel inspired by their presence as you thought you would. Why? It has nothing to do with you, but everything to do with them. A person who doesn't feel good within transmits that poor inner feeling outward, and you feel it.

Have you considered that your personality is just what you think yourself to be? It really is!

Revelation

Do you ever wish you could have been born beautiful or handsome? Do negative thoughts about your personal appearance bother you in your daily life? Whenever those thoughts pop into your mind, do not dwell on them. Instead, keep repeating to yourself that your physical appearance — your looks — has nothing to do with your personality... because it really doesn't! It's only a belief you hold, not the truth. A belief can be dropped at any time, and this one is no exception. You can be free of it once you realize what personality truly is.

Your personality is nothing but your self-image: what you think yourself to be. Does this definition surprise you?

Perhaps until now you thought that your personality was something you inherited from your mother, your father, and the rest of your family members. Knowing that your personality is really what you think yourself to be is quite liberating.

If personality is simply what you think yourself to be, then the question becomes, how can you improve it? Well, if you have truly understood, you do not have to "do" anything to improve it. That's right. You already have a great personality. Believing in this simple fact is enough. It's not a false belief, so you're not deceiving yourself by believing yourself to be something which you are not.

Who you truly are — your essence — is unlimited and great in every way. It's the Source. Your happy natural state is your essence. Doesn't every child have a great personality? Isn't every child a great communicator? This is because a child is untouched by ego or insecurities.

When you shift your paradigm of understanding personality you'll experience a miracle. Those who used to believe that they had poor personalities have been instantly transformed. The day following this revelation, when they reported to work or to school, they were surprised when their colleagues complemented them on how smart they looked. Simply dropping all self-imposed and limiting beliefs about personality, and instead holding onto the thought that they have amazing personalities, changed how others viewed them.

Myths

5. It takes time to improve your personality.

 **Reality**

If you have truly understood the previous myth— its reality and revelation— then you understand that it takes no time at all to "improve" your personality. Change your thoughts about yourself and your personality changes. It's that simple. The beauty of this is that it only takes a moment to change your thoughts

Revelation

You may say, "Yes, all this is true, but I've been thinking negatively about myself for so long that I can't change it overnight!"

"I do believe I have a great personality," you say, "but negative thoughts still plague me. What am I supposed to do? What am I doing wrong?"

It really only takes an instant to have a new, sparkling personality, but for some — and you may be one of those individuals — it takes a little longer to transform a deeply embedded belief system. Something blocks your ability to change your thoughts instantaneously.

In order to effectively eliminate this hurdle, you must first learn a little more about how the process works. For those who are self-confident, their self-image automatically improves. How does this happen? Through the self-image virtuous path, outlined below:

Self-Acceptance Self-Respect (Self-Esteem) Self-Confidence (Great Self-Image)

Those who are already confident have unconsciously walked this path. The first step is self-acceptance. It begins the moment you honestly say, "I accept everything in my life right now. I accept my looks, my body, and my upbringing. I accept that I wasn't born with a silver spoon in my mouth. I accept all the hardships I've faced. I accept everything about me. Everything that has happened to me has molded me into the person I am today."

When you're able to honestly practice this radical acceptance you begin to love yourself. Think about it. But more than that, you also begin to respect yourself. This is how the path from self-acceptance to self-respect works. After all, self-respect is synonymous with self-esteem. Self-respect, in turn, leads to self-confidence. Self-confidence helps create a better image of yourself.

But there's also another path far too many tend to tread. This one is a vicious path that only results in a poor self-image and the ultimate belief that you have a poor personality. This path is outlined below:

Self-Rejection Lack of Self-Respect (Poor Self-Esteem) Lack of Self-Confidence (Poor Self-Image)

Which path are you going to follow? The decision is yours. Accepting yourself is the first simple step you can take. By understanding the process, you've automatically placed yourself on the right path. Self-respect and improved self-image are sure to follow. Remember, it takes only a moment to accept yourself, to feel good about yourself. If you truly understand and believe this, you really need no time at all in order to improve your self-image or uncover your true personality.

Myths

6. If I tell myself I have a great personality then I have an ego problem.
7. Having self-respect is being egotistic.
8. Improved self-respect or a good personality is bad for spiritual growth

Reality

Somewhere along the line, society has led you to believe that if you consider yourself to possess a good personality, then you must be egotistic. Let's set the record straight right now: tell yourself, and truly believe, that this does not make you arrogant.

There's a big difference between self-respect and ego. Self-respect is born from self-acceptance and feeling good about yourself from the inside out. Egotism comes from a place that is outside of your true inner feelings. Unhealthy ego is further illustrated in this section's Revelation.

If you fail to understand the difference, confusion certainly can result. Many misinterpret the predominant idea behind spirituality and its pursuit of an egoless state, and think spirituality requires thinking, "I am nobody. I am nothing compared to others." Maybe you have been led to think that you should have no self-respect at all. That is absolutely not where a true spiritual quest leads. In fact, a person finds their true Self in the spot where there is neither ego nor an inferiority complex.

Revelation

If you have a healthy respect for yourself, you only need to begin to take the proper steps. Once you do this, you will see a tremendous surge of improvement in all areas of your life. Self-respect is actually a valuable asset.

You will even discover a difference in your eating habits. You will eat only as much as you need to fulfill your immediate needs. You will naturally become careful about your diet because you know that eating more than what your body needs can be harmful. This habit is in contrast to the one who is arrogant, or who operates out of ego.

An egotistical person is compelled to impress those around him. "See how great I am? The cake was given to all, but I got more because I am better than all of you. You know, they treat me in a special way here." The egotistical individual wants to show off how much of a VIP he really is. He believes, and tries to make others believe, that he deserves to receive more than everybody else.

In fact, he will go one step further in demanding more food than everyone else. As a result, he will also eat more than he really needs. The egotistical individual continues to eat even though his body signals to his brain that it's satisfied. He may even make himself sick through overeating, but he refuses to drop his ego and admit that he is full. Instead, he eats all the more. Why? He will simply do this to impress those around him. Don't mistake over indulgence for a sign of respect. He respects neither himself nor others.

It is similar to the story of the self-absorbed politician who visited a government official and was kept waiting in the lobby. As you have probably already guessed, he believed a man of his stature should be attended to immediately. In effect, his ego was hurt. He informed the receptionist, "I am not used to being kept waiting." The receptionist remained polite and replied, "Sir, you will have to wait for a while. You can make yourself comfortable in that chair until then." The politician lashed out in anger, "Don't you know who I am? I'm a politician." The receptionist replied casually, "In that case, Sir, you can sit on two chairs." Ego can sometimes loom so large that even if one chair is sufficient you demand two.

The basis of any egotistical thinking is the individual's belief that he is inherently better than others. His line of thinking continues as such: "By being different from others, I gain respect. People may hate me, but I don't really care. I hate them as well. As long as they know that I am superior, I really don't care."

He should be told, "Even if you think you're different from others, stop harboring hatred towards them. Hatred will only sink you into the depths of misery. Even if you believe you're superior, don't put others down. Comparing yourself with others to prop up your ego will only make you burn in the hellfire of jealousy and anger. If you respect yourself, there is a possibility that you may drop this egotistic behavior."

When you respect yourself, your outward actions reflect your inward respect. You will be motivated to attain the supreme truth as soon as possible. In this way, you can see that having self-respect is actually a valuable asset. Self-respect is the necessary beginning of understanding the essence of who you are.[1] With self-respect, the urge to know the answer to the question "Who am I?" increases. The quest begins.

The ego may not disappear overnight. You won't know, nor are you expected to know, who you truly are in the initial stages of this journey. If, however, you begin the process of respecting yourself, you're starting off on the right foot. You have the advantage of beginning with good intentions, and that makes all the difference.

An individual will never respect others until he learns to respect himself. Soon, you will find yourself saying, "I should seek the company of good people because I want to give the best to myself." These are good intentions that spring naturally from self-respect.

But there is a fine line that you have to tread... or else, before long, you may find your healthy respect slowly transforms into an unhealthy ego. Or, if you misinterpret the directive to avoid arrogance, you may err in a different direction. In turn, you lose a certain amount of respect for yourself. When you have a healthy feeling for the true and balanced

---

[1]*In order to have a firsthand experience of who you truly are, you are encouraged to attend the Maha Aasmani Param Gyan retreat organized by Tej Gyan Foundation. Details are provided in the pages at the end of the book.*

meaning of self-respect, you become aware that you are neither superior nor inferior to anyone. You begin to respect yourself as you truly are. By doing so, you will gain a necessary component to Self-realization and come closer to the Truth.

If you do otherwise you will become your worst enemy. Anything other than respecting your true Self only takes you down the path of destruction, leaving you mired in illusion and preventing you from ever attaining the Truth. It will not be long before you may develop bad habits due to the disrespect you feel for yourself.

Imagine for a moment that you've been hurt by someone you respect. Because of your bruised ego you may begin to dislike or even hate him. It is tempting to say, "I'm going to set my respect aside for the moment. Instead, I'll teach him a lesson." As you can plainly see, this in no way expresses any respect for the other person.

In order to remove the ego from your system you have to first acknowledge its existence. The simplest way to do this is to ask yourself, "What is the best method of removing the ego? Do I need any specific knowledge in order to break the ego?" Only individuals with self-respect will begin to entertain such thoughts. You will realize hatred can neither break the ego nor dispel jealousy. Only self-respect can.

A healthy self-respect results in surprising physiological benefits as well. It can help you to break free from many of the physical illnesses that may be plaguing you. When you respect yourself you will not eat more than you can chew. As you recall, those who do not respect themselves tend to overeat. They may even begin to live to eat instead of eating to live. If you currently find yourself eating too much, ask yourself if this is because of arrogance. Make a vow to respect yourself, correct the situation, and eat in moderation.

This is self-esteem, true self-respect. This is the beginning of the journey to reach the Ultimate Truth; for attaining Self-realization. Thus, your spiritual quest begins. Understand that until you attain Self-realization, the ego remains with you. Thus in this journey from self-acceptance to self-respect or self-esteem to self-confidence, the ego will appear time and again.

 **Myths**

9. I am afraid of addressing . large groups of people.
10. Successful individuals don't experience stage fright.
11. I am one of the few people in the entire world who gets stage fright.
12. One day my stage fear will go away. If I really try, it's possible to get rid of stage fright.

 **Reality**

Believe it or not, stage fright is a normal reaction when addressing groups or performing in front of audiences. Everybody on earth has had stage fear at one time or another. You are not alone.

 Revelation

First you need to understand that stage fright is not bad, and can actually work as your ally. A watch works because of the tension created when you wind it. If there were no tension, it would not work. In the same way, stage fear is the positive tension that helps you to prepare. You can turn stage fright into what is called a "positive fear". The tension you feel can propel you to a better and more accurate performance.

Consider the fear of examination which afflicts many students, perhaps even yourself. This fear propels you to study, and motivates you to perform better.

Think about how you would feel if you were to come face to face with a lion. You would be gripped by fear — and plenty of it, guaranteed. Fear pumps adrenalin throughout your body that makes you run like you've never run before. Fear is absolutely necessary in that situation. In fact, it's the driving force that may very well save your life.

Problems arise, however, when the positive tension or fear turns negative, and necessary fear turns into unnecessary fear. This happens when a student is so fearful of his exams that he has nightmares and is unable to study at all. It's like sitting at home and fearing a lion. In a very real sense, you're creating a mental movie of being confronted by a lion. Your body releases adrenalin and other chemicals as if you were really facing a lion, but as there is no lion there is no need to run. Since you do not run, the chemicals are not utilized and instead are converted into toxins. The bottom line is that unnecessary fear eventually transforms itself into physical disease.

You may counter this argument by commenting, "I'm not fearful of the lion. I'm afraid of speaking to a large group." The situation may be different, but the physiological process is the same. You've built up so much fear over the potential of facing an audience that your nervousness shows up as sweaty palms and stuttering or stammering when you speak. Even your mind blanking out is an outward sign of your inward fear.

The answer to your stage fright is quite simple: you need to just work with it. Instead of building up your fear and believing it to be detrimental to your presentation, think the opposite. Don't overreact. Embrace your fear. Remind yourself that it is necessary for doing a good job. Use it to your advantage.

The second important point concerning stage fright is that you are not the only one who experiences it. Every good actor experiences it. The best of speakers will willingly acknowledge that they too still feel this same nervousness as they step to the podium. Even professional speakers experience at least an initial bout of fear. You may think that an individual who is about to give his one thousandth speech would be calm, cool and collected. While he may appear so externally, chances are he was just as nervous as you are now when he gave his first speech many years ago.

When you believe yourself to be the only one who feels stage fright you magnify your fear. Once you realize that everyone else around you is just as nervous and fearful of standing before a group of people as you are, you will be able to accept your fear more openly. When you accept your fear you can make it work for you. You will feel better and more confident.

The third point you should know about stage fright is that it's not curable. If you've lived with this fear for any length of time, you may have already discovered this. You may have already tried many tricks or tips to alleviate it, only to learn that nothing chases it off. Given that this is the case, what do you need to do? For that matter, what do these seemingly confident speakers do?

The answer will surprise you. They have learned to ignore it. Let's face it — there's no benefit to worrying about a problem that is not only universal, but incurable as well.

Let's illustrate this by comparing a confident speaker and a not-so-confident speaker. Both feel nervous in the first few minutes of their speech. The confident speaker knows that this fear is a normal part of his job and there is no cure for it, so he ignores the butterflies in his stomach. He continues performing in spite of it. In contrast, the not-so-confident speaker fears his fear, and allows it to hinder his performance. He stops and stutters and mutters what he did not want to utter.

Confident speakers have ignored their stage fright so many times that it no longer bothers them. They learned not only how to handle the fear, but how to make it work for them. In order to become a confident speaker you too need to face your fear, and step onto that stage again and again. This is how all confident speakers gained their confidence.

The key is to find as many opportunities as you can to speak up, and get yourself used to it. The secret of public speaking is consistency. You may not have expected this advice, but it's the truth. Dive right in, and accept invitations and opportunities to speak in public as often as possible. Give a toast at a dinner, give a speech on your campus corner, or volunteer to speak when someone retires in your office. It's certain that you're beginning to get the idea. Do whatever it takes to stand in front of a group of people. It may be only a small group initially, but even that builds confidence.

If you don't see an opportunity to speak in front of a group, then create one. Organize a group of friends and present a topic to them. Tell your teacher in school that you'd like to make a presentation on a topic. Tell your boss at your workplace that you want to make a presentation. Don't allow your perceived lack of opportunities become an excuse for not speaking. Gain the necessary experience to build your confidence to work with your stage fright, keeping in mind that it will always be with you.

Do not underestimate the power of this strategy. Make it a habit. The confidence you'll receive each time you face a crowd is enormous.

Eventually, you'll admit to yourself, "If I can face fifty new people, I can surely face my dad too." Or you will finally come to realize, "If I can stand up in front of strangers, I can face my boss too." Increase your confidence by facing crowds step by step.

Myths

13. I must eliminate all nervousness so that I can appear confident.
14. I have to first change my thoughts about confidence so that my body language appears confident.
15. I must feel confident first, and then I can act confidently.

Reality

This may seem like a logical progression: first you overcome fear, nervousness, and thoughts of failure, and then you will be confident. However, in reality it works the other way around. Your first step is to alter your body language. At this point you may not believe it, but how you move your body actually determines your moods. This includes your posture, which additionally helps to direct your thoughts. The sooner you start displaying confidence the sooner you will acquire it, even when you do not feel it. Don't wait for your confidence to build. The only sure way to gain the confidence you want is to start living, sitting, walking, working, speaking, and listening with confidence.

This means to be conscious of how you are moving your body as often as possible. For example, whenever you sit, ask yourself, "How am I sitting?" If you believe it is not the way one who believes in himself would sit, then adjust your position immediately. Sit as though you're ready for anything and everything to come to you. Open both your hands and try to feel what the happiness of self-confidence is like. Do this while you are walking, speaking, and working. Whenever you feel closed, straighten your shoulders, raise your head, puff up your chest, and look up to life. Act as if you are royalty.

If you're going for an interview and aren't feeling very confident, all you have to do is to move faster. Yes, even this helps. As you enter the room to face the interview, walk slightly faster than you usually do. Any small change in your body language will make you feel a surge of confidence.

Although it is true that action follows feelings, it's also true that feelings follow action. Act confident and you shall soon feel confident too.

Revelation

Let's do a small exercise to understand the full implications of these seemingly minor changes. As you are reading this chapter, take inventory of yourself. How is your posture? If you feel stressed at this moment, change your posture. Relax. Next, put your hands in the direction of the sky with your palms up. Tell yourself that you are now open to receive all the blessings and confidence that life offers. Feel the happiness, the pleasure of opening up. Remain in this posture for 30 seconds. Now put your hands down.

Did you feel more relaxed? Did you feel open? Of course you did. Practice this in times of stress throughout the day.

If you were asked to do this exercise while you were with other people, how would you have felt? Would you have hesitated? Would you have felt strange? It's not unusual to feel awkward, even fearful, of performing such an exercise in a crowd. If there are 600 people you feel that 1200 eyes are piercingly looking at you.

Your confidence naturally tends to wane a bit. Throughout our various experiences, we don't always get enough opportunities to blossom and open up. Nor do we always talk openly, or walk without fear that others are watching and scrutinizing our every move. If you would feel more comfortable starting with smaller incremental steps, then do so. You might even start by making body language changes that others may not even notice.

Every time you change your body language consciously, ponder the following questions:

1. Did you feel good after you altered your body language? Did you feel the confidence from within?
2. Did you feel more open following the change?
3. Did you feel less constricted and less constrained?

The purpose of this exercise is simple: begin to act the way you want to be. Change your body language and experience a rush of confidence. Now that you are well on your way to challenging and overcoming your beliefs concerning confidence, are you ready to tackle some myths about relationships as well?

■ ■ ■

SECTION III

Demystifying Relationships

7
Myths about Love

T he essence of true love has been lost in the clouds of attachment, infatuation, and lust. We will understand some myths about love in this chapter.

Myths

1. I have to get love.
2. Love is about getting attention.
3. The more we receive love, the more we feel it.

Reality

Though it may sound counter intuitive, "Love" is the only thing that you get by giving rather than by receiving.

In ignorance people focus exclusively on receiving love, because it seems logical that anything that is received increases in quantity. After all, if you received a paycheck every week from your employer and didn't spend any of it, you would have a nice sum of money at the end of the year. You may feel that you may lose something by giving it away. That's why people are ready to receive, but not prepared to give. When one applies this same type of thinking to love, it backfires. People who think and act this way always feel a dearth of love in their lives.

From childhood people learn by watching and then patterning their actions after others. People eventually learn to harbor preconditions: "If the other person gives me this, then I will do that." They don't realize that holding onto their preconditions only distances them from true love. Once they have become distanced in this fashion, they lose opportunities to be made aware of this unintended error in their approach towards life.

Revelation

Love generates an enormous power within each of us. This power propels us to rise beyond our limitations and negative patterns and to act for a higher cause. Love, then, can completely transform us. It gives us the strength to change ourselves, and the motivation to counteract our own limiting habits. The highest sacrifice becomes easy when it's performed in the name of true love.

It's very important that one understands this truth: when love is given unconditionally, one receives it in abundance. Let love be within you and around you, so that its boundless possibilities unfold before you. When one begins to understand the true meaning of love, all the associated false and impure beliefs associated with it are removed.

Myths

4. Jealousy is a different name for love.
5. Jealousy is a sign of exclusive love and caring.

Reality

When some people enter a relationship they believe that the bond of love is exclusively for the two of them. They become attached to each other. They constantly live in fear that the other person might develop a relationship with any third person. No external person is allowed in their territory. They become obsessed and infatuated. This situation and thinking may be taken to such an extent that they don't want the other person even looking at or talking to a third person.

One may feel that there is nothing wrong in being jealous; that it's a sign of exclusive love and caring. As long as it is inspiring you, it's fine. But there's a very fine line between jealousy and ill-will. Slowly, with time, the inspiring aspect of jealousy fades away and can be replaced by a sense of possessiveness and need for control. This is irrational jealousy and it interferes in love. You feel that if you don't have a particular item, your partner should also not have it. You expect the partner to sacrifice his or her areas of interest and align with your interests out of love. At this juncture egos clash, and it results in differences over trivial matters. If you love somebody you'll want that person to be happy, not only in your relationship but in general. You'll want them to be happy, regardless of whether that's with family and friends, in a career, or at school.

Revelation

True love is unconditional when you love someone regardless of the person's behavior. True love can never be experienced by expecting love and attention; it is experienced only by giving love. Even if the other person doesn't pay attention to you, you continue to love unconditionally. You don't need to employ the force that emerges from jealousy or ill-will to attract that person towards you. True love is complete in itself.

 Myths

6. Love is blind.
7. Love is sweet poison.

People use terms like these to describe love out of ignorance and misunderstanding. Those who express love in these terms suffer the outcomes of selfish — that is, conditional — love. There are many songs and poems depicting the tragic outcomes of conditional love, and these songs gain popularity because people appreciate lyrics that mirror their own feelings. The very fact that they are lamenting the outcome only demonstrates that their love was indeed conditional, temporary, and transactional. People ignore this fact, either out of ignorance or other reasons, and then adapt and follow these ideas blindly.

Idioms such as "love is blind" or "love is sweet poison" carry no truth. However, they are heard repeatedly, believed by people who feel that they use their heart more than their head, and become ingrained in their worldview.

 **Myths**

8. Love diminishes with time.

 **Reality**

Only selfish or conditional love is lost with time. Unconditional love, also called bright love, doesn't fade with time. Even during the most strenuous, demanding circumstances, true love never diminishes.

At the beginning of a romantic relationship lovers usually develop an attachment for the physical body. This is conditional love. It's temporary. We all know physical features change with time.

 **Revelation**

We can find many examples of unconditional love that grows with time in history, legend, and religion. Examples are the immortal friendship between Krishna and Sudama, and the devotion symbolized by Radha, Meera, and Rabiya. There is also the love between Master and disciple exemplified by Ramakrishna Paramhansa and Swami Vivekananda.

 Myths

9   Feelings of insecurity, . hatred, and jealousy are found more often in women than men

 **Reality**

By nature a woman's body is usually physically weaker than that of a

man. Due to this physical difference women are more prone to feelings of insecurity based on the need for physical protection. Nature has endowed women with this feeling to aid in avoiding dangerous situations. The stronger the body, the less need there is for the feeling of insecurity.

Today, as women harbor this feeling of insecurity, they may wish to have a separate house of their own to have a shelter to fallback on in case of any problem. Many times hatred is a by-product of this feeling of insecurity

Revelation

It's this way for many reasons, including the way women are brought up, the kind of values and beliefs nurtured in them by their parents and environment, as well as the outlook society has towards them. All of these factors, in many cases, have aggravated this feeling of insecurity. This is the situation as of date. But as women become stronger in many different ways, this feeling can completely vanish in the future.

■ ■ ■

8
Myths about Marriage

U nderstanding some of the myths surrounding marriage will allow us to more fully understand the institution itself.

 **Myths**

1. A woman's name should be changed immediately after her marriage

 **Reality**

The following may be the reasons why this myth came into existence:

a) After marriage a young woman leaves her parents' house and stays at her husband's place. She needs to develop new relationships in that new location and environment. It's like a rebirth. Keeping this in mind, her name is changed so that she can begin her life afresh from that point onwards.

b) Calling her by her former name may remind her of her old relationships which may make her sad. This may create a hurdle for her in settling down into her new home comfortably.

 **Myths**

2. Listening to or telling stories can cause problems with your maternal relatives

Reality

Listening to stories is normally done during free time. For the most part, the activity prompts feeling of relaxation, and even lethargy.

Reading books helps one to fall asleep at night. Additionally, stories act like a lullaby for children. Therefore, it's customary to tell stories at bedtime so that children fall asleep. Sometimes, though, children want to be entertained with these wonderful stories throughout the day.

The time from morning until evening is normally designated as the period for getting work done. Listening to or reading stories may hinder the

accomplishment of that goal. Hence, this myth was developed to prevent children from habitually demanding stories throughout the day, and to free adults for work during working hours.

 Myths

3. A young man born under a specific position of Mars in the natal chart (manglik) should only marry a woman who also has a similar astrological chart.
4. It is necessary to match horoscopes to ensure a good marriage.
5. The positions of stars and planets affect us so strongly that we are like puppets when it comes to our behavior at certain times of the year.

Reality

People born on different days under different configurations of stars have different physical and mental constitutions. If people with compatible constitutions are paired, their marriages have a better chance at lasting long. On the other hand, pairing people with identical constitutions may cause problems. If both are aggressive, for example, the marriage may dissolve in arguments and fights. If both are spendthrifts the family may develop financial problems. If both are misers their children will have to suffer. Therefore, their natures should complement each other for the sake of harmony. If one person has an angry disposition, their partner must be serene and understanding; if one is an extrovert, the other should be an introvert.

However, it's not absolutely necessary that those with similar planetary positions only marry each other. Regardless of the planetary positions on the individuals' astrological charts, ultimately it is their mindsets that matter in the creation of a lasting marriage. It's not a wise move to seek advice from astrology.

Revelation

It certainly is true that the stars and planets exert a certain amount of effect on each one of us. However, that can also be said about the thoughts of different people on earth. Even more so, the earth also has its effect on us. Everything in this world has some type of an effect on us; yet that does not mean it hampers our expression. For the most part, all of these variable factors merely support us. How would we walk if the earth was not pulling us down?

The effect, therefore, is always there... but has no one questioned as to how much? Actually, our thoughts are by far the largest influence upon us. Therefore, once we change our thoughts, other variables will begin to support us. You'll find that you'll have fewer roadblocks in your path when you start by changing your thinking.

We've all learned in school that our body contains a certain percentage of water. Outside factors affect the behavior of water. Think of the high and low tides of the sea, or the effects of the phases of the moon on bodies of water. Similarly, the water content that flows inside our body is affected by outside forces. It simply makes sense that at times we are energetic and at other times we're depressed or lethargic. These phases are temporary and transitory; do not consider them to be blockages.

Our ancestors envisioned the far-reaching consequences of these beliefs. They anticipated problems stemming from the belief that for those born under a specific position of Mars, whatever unfortunate event has to occur must happen to the first wedded. Therefore, they suggested including a pot in the wedding of people in this situation. Thus, the misfortune would happen to the pot. Once the pot was "married" it was broken, signifying the end of its life. This custom helped to change people's beliefs, as well as their thinking, about those born under a certain astrological sign or zodiac constellation.

■ ■ ■

9
Myths about Parenting

A ll parents have rules for themselves and make rules for their children, both explicit and assumed. A worldview framed by these rules may lead them to say, or think to themselves, statements such as:

> My neighbor's son is a bully: he got into an argument with my little son!
>
> Don't break your toys! Be a good boy!
>
> I am your father and I always know what's best for you.
>
> We should never argue in front of our children. It's easier to raise girls than boys.
>
> Parenting was easier when I was a teen. Today's teens are difficult to handle!

What leads us to the rules that inspire these statements? The simple answer is the collection of beliefs and myths that have grown around parenting. Listed below are some deep-rooted myths that you may hold as a parent. Ask yourself if you consider these statements to be true, as they may actually be limiting your ability to be a great parent.

Myths

1. The child is too young to understand anything. You don't have to take children seriously. Children don't get hurt emotionally.

Reality

While it is true and widely acknowledged that one should not physically harm a child, many parents end up causing far more dangerous emotional harm than they could imagine. Children are very sensitive and understand things we say to them. As parents, we must safeguard our children from both physical and emotional abuse. Be mindful of what you say to them.

Revelation

The best way to explain this is through an example. A child hears his mother say, "Today we are going to have some relatives visit us. Be on your best behavior." In the evening the child sees the relatives arrive at his home. The child is impressed. A few days later, the mother says, "It is going to rain tonight." It rains that night and the child is impressed again. He thinks whatever his mother says will come true. One day, the child does something that upsets the mother. The mother scolds him and says, "You are hopeless and good for nothing." What do you think the youngster's reaction to this will be? Based on his mother's spotless track record of what he considers predictions, he automatically believes whatever his mother says. He remembers this sentence for a long time and incorporates it into his beliefs about himself. He grows up to be a person who lacks confidence, is always subdued, doubts his own decisions, and lives a depressed life.

Myths

2. I will love my child the way I wish my parents had loved me.
3. I will love my child exactly how my parents loved me.

Reality

The needs of every child are different. Each child has an individual love bank and needs it to be full every moment. Some children like to be cuddled by their parents; their parents' touch makes them feel comfortable and secure. Some children want parents to play with them; they feel loved when their parents give them attention. Others need gifts; they love to be with their toys and gadgets. Others like to gain and share knowledge with parents; they overwhelm their parents with questions. Before you can show your child the type of love he or she needs, you should know what type of child you're dealing with. If you try to shape them to your own personal ways of thinking they might resist or get subdued. Worse yet, they may never explore all their possibilities. Your perception of what your child needs might be different than what the child truly needs. Understand your children's needs, and give them what they need accordingly.

 **Myths**

4. Don't . be strict with your children.
5. Don't shower too much love upon your children.

 **Reality**

According to traditional roles, a father is supposed to give a child the hardware (hard training) and a mother is supposed to give the child software (soft love). Both tough love and soft love are required, along with wisdom, to make children into better individuals.

 Myths

6. Parenting is tough, the hardest job in the world. It's better to not be a parent or commit to parenting.
7. What's the point of parenting if your children will not care for you when they grow up?

Reality

Parenting is the divine task of shaping the character of a child. It's the enjoyable task of giving to the world someone who will make the world an even better place. It's also a way to uncover the qualities of compassion, care, and patience within yourself. The very purpose of parenting is to release unconditional love within you.

 **Myths**

8. The primary responsibility of parents is ensuring that their children are advancing academically.

 **Reality**

The primary responsibility of a parent is to cultivate or pass on positive values to their children. As a parent, you should prioritize character-building over all else

Revelation

Every child is like a white board, and the parents are the markers that write on the board. The child will act and live his or her life according to what is written on the board. While academic excellence should be one of the key aspects of your child's growth, the most important responsibility of a parent is to show children the path to holistic growth so they become complete individuals.

 Myths

9. Teach your children spiritual . values and morality from a young age by telling them about spirituality and explaining scriptures to them.

Reality

Don't teach spirituality to your children by relying on words —demonstrate spirituality to them. The best thing you can give to your children is the gift of happiness and peace. Let your children see how you make decisions with inner peace and how you act with inner poise, and these qualities will be transferred to them. Giving children spiritual instructions at a young age may confuse them.

If you want to instruct children, do so by self-development. Teach them concentration, willpower, focus, communication, and other skills along these lines. Talk to them about strength, stamina, and taking initiative. Verbalize skills for your children, but let them internalize spiritual wisdom by observing you.

Revelation

Parents leave a lasting impression of their actions on their children. Your child — as all children do — replicates what he or she observes, becoming a photocopy of you. At every moment children are absorbing some aspect of the actions, words, behavioral patterns, and habits of their parents, relatives, and teachers. Children are not capable of analyzing or contemplating at a young age, but simply and unquestioningly accept their observations as facts.

Visualize for just a moment, if you can, what image your children will try to create when they become parents. They will fill their children with the same beliefs and myths they lived with all their lives. They will transfer all their patterns and tendencies to their children. A child does not differentiate between right and wrong in their actions, but thinks whatever parents do is correct and the right way to live.

Myths

10. I must ensure my children have access to the best education and become intelligent and smart.

Reality

While it's right to want the best education for your child, the best gift a parent can give a child is to teach them the art of learning. The art of learning helps them to explore greater heights in life. The art of learning can then be applied not only to academics, but other aspects of life — social, physical, emotional, financial, and spiritual — all of which together lead to a complete life. Teach your child to learn, and show him or her how to lead a spiritual and moral life by observing you. There can be no better gift than teaching your children to break themselves free of the miseries of life and to achieve the ultimate goal of their purpose on this earth.

Myths

11. I was responsible for bringing my children into this world; therefore I should worry about them.
12. I own my children. At least, I own my children while they are in my home. As long as they live with me, they should only do what I say.

Reality

A parent's concern for a child is natural, but it should not turn into worry. Let your concern be a happy concern, if you can imagine that. But do not worry. Know that it's God's will, and these challenges have come into your life to make you stronger and wiser. When you tackle life's challenges with happiness, you become a magnet for positivity and attract nothing but the best things into your life. When you worry unnecessarily, you lose your ability to attract the best and become like a worthless piece of brass.

Revelation

Khalil Gibran says, "Your children come 'through' you, not 'from' you." You do not own your children. Neither do you owe them anything. You only own your response towards them, and your response tells you whether you are parenting effectively or not.

■ ■ ■

SECTION IV
Demystifying Death

10
Myths about Death and related Rites and Rituals

Perhaps no other aspect of life is shrouded in as many myths, rites, and rituals as death. As often as we acknowledge that death is a part of life, we still tend to confine it to a corner all its own. Every religious organization has its own rituals. Every family has certain rites they follow when a family member dies. Where did these rites and rituals come from, and why? In this chapter, we'll discuss some of the most common myths, rites, and rituals related to death.

 **Myths**

1. Women shouldn't be allowed in a crematorium.

This superstition is based in beliefs about the nature of women. Some individuals say that women are emotional by nature, and contend that women are frightened when they see tragedy, injuries, suffering, or a dead body. Sometimes when a dead body is cremated, because of heat, the bones start deforming and bending, and it appears as though the body is moving. This superstition was made to protect women from such frightening images

---

 **Myths**

2. A son must shave his head following the death of his father or an elderly family member.

Historically this custom has been an outward indication of a death in the family. This is a signal to others to treat the family members with sympathy. Secondly, it reminds the son of his increased family responsibilities

Revelation

It does not matter whether a son shaves his head or not. The state of mind of family members and relatives is more important than external appearances.

 **Myths**

3. While leaving . a place where death has occurred, one should never say, "I am going."

 **Reality**

The reason for this myth is simple: the statement "I am going" may only aggravate the grief of the people present. In that distressing situation, someone may ask, "Are you going to leave me too?"

 **Revelation**

If you need to leave the place, then do so without saying anything. If you must say something, then say, "I will be back" or "See you again." This conveys the message that you aren't leaving forever; you will be back soon.

 **Myths**

4. Water from the holy river . Ganges (or any other holy river) should be sprinkled on a person returning from a crematorium. You should take a bath when you return from a funeral.

 **Reality**

In many religions, it is customary for a person returning from a crematorium, or a place where death has occurred, to be sprinkled with water or to take a bath. A person returning from a crematorium may have come into contact with germs. A sprinkling of river water or turmeric water will cleanse the person of these germs.

After a funeral, the process of bathing indicates that our relationship with the deceased is over. In this way, all negative thoughts are symbolically washed away. Many of the rituals performed at a crematorium are done so that people can live their lives without fear in the future.

Revelation

Any sort of cleansing of the body is recommended after visiting a crematorium

Myths

5. In a family where death has taken place, a shraadh (a Hindu ceremony performed every year in which offerings are made to Brahmins and cows in honor of ancestors) must be arranged so that the offerings can reach the person for whom they are intended.
6. After someone dies in a family, other family members are required to perform certain rituals.

Reality

People fear the ghosts of the dead, and so they perform various religious ceremonies and rituals in order to frighten the ghosts away. In reality there is no such thing as ghosts, and so there is no question of them getting frightened. The real purpose of those ceremonies is to help us rid ourselves of fears, and in the process become more confident. Rituals concerning the dead do not affect the dead, but they definitely affect us. These ceremonies were created and are conducted in order to prevent us from becoming receptive to negative energies, and to make our thoughts positive.

Rituals are also performed as a safety or a precautionary measure. If a corpse is kept too long then worms may breed in it, and so certain rituals are followed for the sake of health and cleanliness. Similarly, purification rites are performed at the place where the dead body is kept or where the body is burnt.

Those who have not treated their elders well may perform these ceremonies after their elders' deaths to rid themselves of guilt. Others teach their children to continue these practices out of fear, because they believe if their children do not perform the rituals then they will suffer in the afterlife. Not everyone performs the ceremonies for reasons like these. The main purpose of these rituals, though, is to help us pray for the person who has passed away, to help the soul's onward journey.

Considering this background information, it's easy to see why people perform various rituals prescribed by their religions. With understanding, performing some rituals immediately after the death of a loved one may be beneficial to the living. However, several rituals performed for the first eleven months are unnecessary.

Revelation

Ceremonies and rituals were not created to get rid of ghosts, and such rites do not have anything to do with the person who has passed. These rituals are conducted, for the most part, to help the relatives of the deceased during a very trying period.

Some people perform a collective prayer, or organize a condolence meeting. Collective prayer is very powerful. In fact, prayer should be the only purpose behind any ritual concerning the deceased. If this is happening, then the ritual is worthwhile. Otherwise, merely overcrowding people in a room is of no value. It is also useless to pray or to do anything out of fear, or inorder to inflate self-image.

If performing rituals brings happiness to those close to the deceased, then certainly perform them. Keep in mind, though, that none of these ceremonies are necessarily essential. You can send the departed off with a simple prayer, and pray for those relatives remaining on this plane.

 **Myths**

7. Euphemisms must be used when a person dies. Instead of saying that a man is dead, it is said that God has chosen him or called him up, that he has gone to the other world, that he has become a resident of heaven, and so on.

These euphemisms are used to avoid confusion. If people are told the truth, that the physical body of the person has perished but the soul is still continuing the journey, they will become bewildered. When someone dies there are all kinds of people affected, including children, and not all of them are able to understand weighty concepts. In addition, under stressful circumstances not all are prepared to listen to the real answer. Therefore, euphemisms are used to keep everyone calm in the distress that follows a death.

When someone dies we feel sorrow and pity, and wonder what their life would have been like. Certain rituals are performed in an attempt to find out. People also think about which world he must have reached, and consult different people to find the answer. But no one is able to give the right answer. Instead, they give the same ready-made answers that their predecessors have handed down to them over generations.

Some expressions are generally used to soothe and comfort those who remain after a loved one has departed. Relatives and friends want nothing more than reassurance that their near and dear one has a good life after death. These sayings help to do just that. Some of the standard sayings are: "He has gone to the shelter of God"; "God has chosen him and called him"; "He is now residing in heaven"; "He is happy there"; and so on.

Anything negative uttered may upset the distressed relatives. Only good things are said about the deceased, and anything bad is avoided, so as to avoid hurting anybody's feelings. Therefore, taking all these factors into consideration, euphemisms and positive words are used when talking about the deceased.[2]

Myths

8. If someone has helped you or served you selflessly, then you should offer him the "thanks-giving" or gratitude prayer after his death.

Reality

In the act of thanksgiving, regardless of the type or how small or large, the person who is offering the thanks is really the one who benefits. The habit of thanking is vital. It's also the genesis of this myth. When you offer a prayer of thanksgiving to the departed, that seemingly small act helps you to feel better. You establish a feeling of gratitude instead of grieving. You can use any kind of words in your prayer, but regardless of which words you use, they should be filled with deep feeling.

If you continue to remember the deceased and recall the good deeds that he has done, that too is a form of prayer. It's a misconception that prayer can only be offered using words. If you feel thankful to the one who has departed and say a few words about him, that too is a prayer. If you talk about the good things he had done during his lifetime, then that is also a kind of prayer. Remembering good things is a prayer because it induces positive feelings in you, which in turn help bring more positive things into your life.

---

[2] *In order to gain more clarity about what exactly happens during death and life after death, please refer to the books titled "Beyond Life" and "Soul Purpose" by Sirshree.*

Revelation

If you feel thankful towards a person, it is very important to let him know about your feelings of gratitude and love while he is still alive. If you don't do this, you may find yourself among those who express their gratitude only after the death of a person. If you do express thanks, your relationship with that person will improve remarkably and become much warmer. The simple phrase "Thank You" is not just a feeling, but a heartfelt cry from deep within. You don't have to use highly ornate words in order to offer this prayer, or to express your gratitude to a person. You don't have to utter special mantras or religious hymns to pray. Words that come from deep within your heart are already prayers.

 Myths

9. One has to go through eighty-four thousand births before one can attain a human birth.
10. Depending on one's karma, one continues to be reborn in various realms in the form of a human, animal, or other creature.

Reality

The belief about rebirth exists to enable man to discharge his present karmas (actions) well. It motivates him to progress farther in his onward journey and enables him to reap good fortune in the future. With careful attention to good karma the highest possibility of Selfrealization and Self-expression can unfold through his body as well. From the perspective of higher consciousness, though, all the births are of the Self (Consciousness) alone.

As you might see, not everyone can understand this higher reality; thus beliefs, rather than the truth, became popular among the masses. Beliefs are relevant at every level according to the level of understanding of a person. As understanding matures an individual can begin to understand the higher answers.

In fact, when the belief about eighty-four thousand births came into place, it was actually referring to eighty-four thousand unique species which existed on earth at that time. Because all the births are assumed by the Self, that belief became popular. Now that the number of species on earth has increased we need to redefine that belief.

Think of Ram enacting the character of Shakuntala on stage. After some time he also plays the role of Shakuni. Would you say that Shakuntala has been reborn as Shakuni? No. The roles of Shakuntala and Shakuni are performed by the same actor, that's all. You can call it a re-birth if you'd like, but it should be understood that it's the same actor playing different roles. At the outset it may appear that a particular person has been re-born, but this is because the memories have been re-used by the Self.

■ ■ ■

SECTION V
Demystifying Divinity

11
Myths about God

Many of us hold myths about God. Changing your thinking about the nature of God and your relationship with Him is difficult for most people. Very likely, when you do this you're asking yourself to change ideas and beliefs you've carried since you were a youngster.

 **Myths**

1. God was born.
2. God was created.

 Reality

We know God created everything, but we keep questioning, "Who created God?" We all know that God cannot die. If He cannot die, then how could He have been born? How could He have been created? Thus the question "Who created God?" is meaningless.

This thinking, while erroneous, is quite understandable. After all, everything we see in this world is based on the Science of the mind. Every single item we see has either been created or invented. When you were in school, you were continually learning about this invention or that discovery being created by a particular scientist, or a manufacturer, or a producer. It is only natural, then, that many keep asking how God was either created or born.

 **Myths**

3. God is male.

 Reality

This is another popularly held but erroneous myth. God is beyond all forms, thinking, and imagination.

The moment you hear the word "God", especially in India, you probably visualize a man wearing many ornaments, a crown, or perhaps holding weapons in either hand. While these portrayals evoke images of how people visualize God, they only hinder the journey of the sincere seeker.

Society has been dominated by males for centuries. Men have been actively involved in the decision-making processes of societies, the politics of communities and nations, and even in the ruling of kingdoms. A male God is simply a natural extension of this concept.

This image, while false, only continues the male dominance that exists. Women, in contrast, have been looked down upon and considered inferior and weak. This has made it even easier to imagine the Almighty in a male form.

What is the color of the sky? You may assume the answer is blue. But a teacher asked his students this question. One student replied, "Yellow." Another one said, "Black." Were they both wrong? Actually, they were both right. The first one based his answer on his observation of the evening sky; the second had seen the night sky. Everybody has a different perception of the same reality. So it is with our images of God.

Perhaps the image of God you have held has actually kept you away from a deeper and fuller relationship with Him. Consider this illustration for a moment. How would you respond if someone asked you the shape of an idli (rice pancake)? You naturally would say it is round. You don't envision a square-shaped idli. But if you did, would that really change the taste of the food? It wouldn't. In fact, you may be surprised to discover that they taste like a round-shaped ones. The bottom line is that your belief is so strong that you believe an idli must be round-shaped, not square.

So it is with your perception of God. When you hear the words "Lord Rama", you immediately recall the image of the actor who played that character in the television serial "Ramayana". The same happens in the case of "Lord Krishna". If you have ever seen the classic English movie "The Ten Commandments", then the voice of God will forever be the actor who played the role. Similar kinds of visualizations and portrayals are seen in calendars and posters of God. If, as a seeker, you use these images as guideposts along your journey, you will never find God.

Revelation

God is beyond gender and cannot be accurately represented by using either

"He" or "She". However, for the sake of convenience and readability, we are using the pronoun "He" in this book.

 Myths

4. God is formless.
5. God has a form, and He looks like this.

 **Reality**

As a human being, you use the only real tools that you have at your disposal — your mind and intellect — to view and understand the world around you. They help you to comprehend both the forms and the formless. God, however, is beyond all forms and shapes, and beyond the mind and the intellect.

Children need pictures to understand words and concepts. Naturally, those beginning their spiritual journey, like children, are shown a picture to help them understand. Considering the needs of their particular time, enlightened masters deliberately created specific pictures of God. They knew that after individuals achieved the full realization of God, these pictures would no longer be required.

Revelation

God is formless, but He needs form to realize Himself. Amongst all the living beings, human form is the only form through which He can know Himself. So He needs a body, just as a person needs a mirror to see himself. Because of this, a beginner naturally asks:

Does God have a form and sometimes become formless?

Is God formless and sometimes assumes a form?

The answer in the second set of circumstances is correct. The average person would prefer ornaments to gold, and considers gold to increase in value when it is made into ornaments. However, for a goldsmith all ornaments are nothing but gold. He sees one in all. Similarly, the average person understands "form" more than what is formless. But just as gold and ornaments are of the same value to a goldsmith, for the wise form and formless are the same.

Let's think of it this way: both individuals who believe that God has form and those that believe God is formless are watching the same movie. One, however, sees the first half of the film which occurs before intermission, while the other sees the part following intermission. After watching the movie they argue to prove each other wrong; but the fact is that both have watched the same movie.

Myths

6. There are many Gods.
7. Each God is different from the others.

Reality

There is only one God. When humans believe that there are many Gods they become entangled in all sorts of beliefs. This only leads to confusion and erroneous ideas, such as: some Gods are uncompromising while some are merciful; eating sour food makes some Gods angry; breaking a fast makes some Gods angry; some Goddesses can enter into a human body and possess it; different Gods like different colors. Such limiting assumptions lead to the bondage of rituals.

Revelation

A seeker who views God in different forms prays to every form differently.

When his prayers do not get answered, his faith begins to wane and his devotion, in turn, wavers. Once he realizes that there is only one God and all the prayers reach one Source (the Self, the Truth, the Almighty), his prayers change. He then prays to the Source. His faith surpasses the assumptions of gender, religion, and form. He begins to believe in the formless, timeless, ageless, and omnipresent. He understands that "Only God exists." Now his prayers flow out of pure devotion and respect, not out of imagination and fear.

 **Myths**

8. God gets angry. We must fear God.

Reality

God is Love. Love cannot get angry.

It's only your limiting beliefs that make you presume that God can become angry. For example, you may believe that if you walk past a temple without bowing down to God or joining your hands in reverence, God gets angry. Man thinks God is like him. Man gets angry, so God must too.

That gives rise to a question: What, then, is the difference between God and man? In a lighter vein, it can be said that God gets angry because humans think that He really does get angry. The fear of God you may carry around with you is absolutely unnecessary. This is a total creation of humankind. People were taught to fear God as a way to make them live a virtuous life and perform good deeds.

What is the actual value of good deeds performed out of fear? Deeds should be done with love, respect, understanding, and devotion. They are far more valuable when performed from this mindset.

Revelation

Fear of God was used early in the history of humankind in an attempt to cope with a callous, uncaring, and unpredictable world. In ancient times people couldn't explain the scientific causes of natural disasters like earthquakes or floods. Because the scientific reasons behind these events remained a mystery, they assumed that these unfortunate events occurred because the gods were upset about something. They turned to the only type of explanation they could understand: the wrath of God. The flashes of lightning during thunderstorms were naturally believed to be the result of God's anger. Simply put, ignorance about nature led to such beliefs. The fear of God is ignorance. Conversely, prayer to God is wisdom, and love for God is Supreme Knowledge.

 Myths

9. God resides within.
10. God resides outside.

Many individuals pray to God believing Him to be outside them. Others believe Him to be inside them. Now, the question arises: which one is right? Does God reside within us or outside of us? The mind supplies the ideas "God is in" or "God is out", because the true idea of God is beyond the grasp of the mind.

We can understand this concept easily with the use of an example. When we deep fry potatoes they are fully immersed in cooking oil. One may ask, "Is the oil present inside the fries, or is it outside?"

The reply is simple: "The fries are within the oil. The oil is inside the fries as well as outside of them." In the same way, we are present within God. God is inside our bodies as well as outside us. In fact, the whole universe is present within God. This means God is everywhere.

The question then arises: "If God is both inside and outside of us, where is it easy to seek Him?" It is easy to seek God inside us, as we are with our bodies all day long. Understand that God is beyond the concepts of "inside" and "outside". God is not in us. We are in God, like fish are in water.

 **Myths**

11. God is in the idol one worships.

God is not in the face of the idol, but in the belief behind the eyes of the person who sees the face of the idol.

Throughout your life, you have undoubtedly lived with beliefs or myths about God which have been passed onto you, without challenging these beliefs. Enlightened souls created idols and analogies as a reminder to explain and understand God. But people have mistaken the idols, the analogies, and the signs of God for God Himself.

Even today, all idols you see, be them of Shiva or Buddha, give you a single message: to go within yourself. Shiva gives the message of the world within. Shakti (Shiva's power or expression) represents the world you see outside of yourself. In a nutshell, Shiva is "Self at rest", or the Reality or the Truth, and Shakti is "Self in action", or Self's creation or the Illusion.

 **Myths**

12. When we go through troublesome or testing situations in life it means God doesn't love us.

Reality

God is love. Love never hates. When people encounter sorrow in life they feel that God doesn't love them. Such feelings arise out of ignorance. The very fact that we are breathing, the immense grace by which we are alive, confirms God's boundless and uncompromising love. But people doubt God due to their skewed definition of love. They feel God's love only when their petty material desires are fulfilled, not otherwise. If you understand that God is "Consciousness" and love is a quality of Consciousness, then this myth will hold no ground

■ ■ ■

12
General Myths about Spirituality

We've just seen a large number of myths that limit true understanding of God. There are just as many false beliefs regarding the topic of spirituality.

 **Myths**

1. To be spiritual you must live To in solitude, in a state of depression, and without any worldly responsibilities.

 **Reality**

Many of us have believed this myth for a long time. But the true nature of spirituality is this: being stabilized in the experience of the Truth, rendering service with the underlying understanding of "Who am I", and being instrumental in spreading Truth and bliss.

Those experiencing true spirituality live in genuine and lasting serenity or calmness. They are not melancholic. They live in happiness and not in sadness. Instead of shirking their responsibilities, they have assumed the highest responsibility that any individual can undertake.

 **Myths**

2. Spirituality means living in solitude, being a recluse.

 **Reality**

Many individuals spend most of their life as one of two extremes. At one end stands the recluse: an individual who runs away from life. He lives alone with minimal contact with others. At the other end stands the householder, the family man (or woman). The householder is completely busy with his family. In fact, his world exclusively revolves around his family.

Be neither a recluse nor a preoccupied householder. Instead, be a bright householder. The bright householder lives within this world, enjoys what the world offers, and spreads joy around. At the same time, he remains detached from the world. He lives a balanced life, without the need to go to either of the extremes.

A bright householder evolves spiritually when he commits himself to live in the world. Nothing is gained spiritually by running away from the world and hiding in the forest. By the same token, nothing is gained by hiding behind the family.

Revelation

A bright householder lives in the world, but at the same time he is detached from the world. He is just like a lotus flower. A lotus flower lies in a pond but can be removed from the pond with ease.

Not only is the bright householder detached from deceit and manipulation, but so are his children, since they are raised with the right understanding. He understands the value of personal relationships. He knows the meaning of bonding in marriage. He is clear that the purpose of a married life is that the husband and wife should become channels of spiritual growth for each other.

Myths

3. Spirituality begins at the age of 50 when one is free from most responsibilities.

The earlier you begin your spiritual growth, the better off you will be. Most people are of the opinion that once a person has reached the age of 50 he begins to settle down. They think he is less attached to life at that age, and so it becomes natural for him to feel a greater pull toward examining his spiritual side.

Perhaps this is true for some individuals, but this isn't always the way it happens. Very often, after the age of 50 physical variables may make spiritual growth more difficult. The body, for example, may be more susceptible to diseases and pain. The appearance of these physical challenges then jeopardizes one's ability to examine his spiritual side. It hinders his contemplation, and even disrupts his meditation.

The body-mind mechanism of an older person is stiffer than that of a younger one. A younger, more flexible body can support a meditation routine with greater ease. For all of these reasons, you should start your spiritual journey as soon as possible.

Revelation

The poet-Saint Dnyaneshwar was enlightened at the age of 16 and took Samadhi (a timeless state of meditation) at the age of 21. Lord Buddha, Saint Kabir, Saint Guru Nanak, Lord Mahavir, and Saint Adi Shankaracharya, to name but a few, are all shining examples of the advantages of beginning the spiritual quest at an early age.

Myths

4. Spirituality is about wearing saffron robes or subscribing to a special dress code.

Reality

The way you dress has no bearing on your spiritual growth. Everyone travels along his own spiritual path. An individual who sincerely seeks the Truth performs some penance at the level of the body or the mind. This penance involves strict control over aspects of body-mind functioning. It involves disciplines such as fasting, contemplation, and meditation. Some seekers utter specific sacred words or mantras, or create visual pictures to help them in their spiritual journey. This is a necessary step in the process in order to help one remember the ultimate purpose.

Some mendicants and seekers choose to wear orange robes. The robe serves as a reminder, not only to the person wearing it, but also to those around him, that he is abstaining from worldly pleasures. This is merely a visual prompt that he should remain detached from the illusory material world (maya). This dress code also allows others to remind him of his purpose if he ever gets attracted to the illusory world.

The tradition of adhering to a simple dress code evolved to help an individual maintain continuity in his contemplation process, as well as to save time. Without this code, a person may spend valuable time in selecting the color, style, and brand of his clothing. The time spent on stitching, laundering, and tending to clothes could otherwise be spent on spiritual matters.

Revelation

To recognize that clothes do not define spirituality is not to discount the fact that what we wear truly has an influence on us. Comfortable clothes, for example, make us feel more at ease and allow us to move in a less inhibited fashion. We walk around more easily and freely. Our body language changes.

Our physical feelings of relaxation get reflected in our thoughts as well.

Colors, too, have an effect on our feelings. Some colors create good feelings and some create bad feelings. For this reason, people value colors more in a spiritual life. Using positive colors and comfortable clothes helps in the initial stages of the journey. After gaining balance in spiritual practice (sadhana), colors or clothes don't make much of a difference.

 **Myths**

5. Spirituality means special ornaments, turning beads, and chanting.

 **Reality**

Turning beads and chanting help the restless mind to settle down. Remember their purpose in contemplation, and work with intention.

Having said that, we must once again consider why rituals were created in the first place. They weren't instituted so we can become enslaved to them. Quite the contrary, they were intended to be outward signals to help us understand the purpose, the Truth. Spirituality is not found in the performance of a ritual.

 Revelation

These reminders of spirituality were devised in the ancient times. Now the times have changed. So, we can also think of choosing new objects or practices as reminders.

 Myths

6. Spirituality is meant for a select few.

 **Reality**

Spirituality is reality, and reality is meant for all. Could there be a person who, despite using a particular object, knows nothing about it, or even cares to know about it? Consider an example: let's say you're using a pen.

Wouldn't you like to know how it writes? How many ink-refills are there inside it, one or more? You probably would like to know everything about it.

Let's say the pen has four refills of different colors, but you use it thinking there is only one refill of one color. When you discover the reality only at the end, wouldn't you have some feelings of regret? You'd think, "If only someone had told me that the pen had four colors! I would have used it to its fullest potential." When you study spirituality, it reveals everything about yourself — all your colors, as it were. This is why it is an essential exercise for all.

Revelation

Spirituality reveals concepts such as:

What is the highest potential of the human body you have received?

What are all the aspects that are present within it?

What is the treasure that lies inside your body?

When you take time to pursue spirituality you are reminded of the treasure within. Every person should know all the possibilities he or she can achieve through the body-mind mechanism. For this reason spirituality is not meant for a select few, but is essential for all.

When you buy a new appliance you first read the instruction manual. Why? Because you'd like to have all the possible information about the appliance that you're about to use. Similarly, you must have complete knowledge about your body-mind mechanism: what it can accomplish, and who you, the one who has received this body-mind mechanism, are in essence. Spirituality gives you information about all of this.

Some people, though, still imagine that spirituality is only meant for those who are miserable and those who want to escape from life without fighting it out. It's time to remove these false concepts from your mind.

 **Myths**

7. Spirituality is weighing every deed to see whether it will lead to hell or heaven.

 **Reality**

First you need to know that hell and heaven are mere reminder systems for those beginning their spiritual journey and still finding their path. Think of how a child is trained: a reward and punishment system ensures the child does his work at home as well as in school.

Most children initially cultivate good habits, develop sound character, and follow a value system due to the fear of punishment. Once the youngsters have grown and matured, that reward and punishment system isn't needed. They understand the importance of these habits without having to have the threat of discipline hanging over them.

In the same way, spiritual beginners are offered the tantalization of heaven and the threat of hell as incentive for proper performance. As long as the underlying understanding is missing from their education, they continue to dwell in the illusions of hell and heaven.

 Revelation

People carry around their own heaven and hell with them. Those who think negatively carry their own personal hell wherever they go. These individuals cannot tolerate good things, and even have the ability to find bad in what is good. When you're around these people you experience exactly what hell is. You try to avoid them whenever possible, or flee when you encounter one.

On the other hand, you enjoy the company of positive thinkers. It feels good just to be around them. When you are around them, you too experience heaven.

 **Myths**

8. The temple bell should be rung when one is entering the temple. It shouldn't be rung when one is leaving the temple.

 **Reality**

The ringing of the bell, while entering a temple, creates an ethereal atmosphere. Its vibrations create an echo in the temple, which helps one to concentrate. It also serves as a reminder to communicate with God and helps one to meditate effortlessly.

However, if the bell is rung while one is leaving the temple, then there is a possibility that the sound will disrupt the state of silence and tranquility. It may cause one to lose the peace of mind gathered inside the temple through contemplation, concentration, meditation, and prayer. This practice was instituted so that the state of silence can be retained even when one has left the temple.

 Myths

9. Never stand on the threshold of a temple.

Reality

This belief originated partly because of the structure of temple doors.

a) *The doorframes of most temples are kept short so that people bow down while entering through them. If someone stands in the doorway he might hit his head.*

b) *Standing in the doorway blocks the view of the idol, which is placed in the innermost sanctum of the temple. Some people, who are in a hurry, wish only to catch a glimpse from outside. They will have difficulty if someone is standing in the way.*

c) *Standing on the threshold is like being on the same platform as God. This act is treated as a symbol of ego.*

 **Myths**

10. You must change your name in order to experience true spiritual growth.

 **Reality**

Some spiritual practices involve a guru or a spiritual master giving his disciple a new name. Having a new name allows the student to feel free from the past. It also inspires enthusiasm to start his or her life afresh.

 Myths

11. One should bow in a temple, otherwise God will get angry.

 **Reality**

The temple is a place where the mind can turn inward. When the mind is constantly focused on outside circumstances it becomes impure and restless. Just as we bathe our body when it's dirty, we need to focus our mind within when it reaches this state. In meditation, when the mind dives inside, it experiences patience and purity. It cleanses itself of all toxins, like deceit and anxiety. After this purifying process the mind can conduct its activities free of contaminating factors. Thus, taking a dip within, into the core of your being, is more important than bowing your body to a physical

structure. Bowing externally before any idol or structure is symbolic of surrendering to pure Consciousness, which is the Source of our existence.

Our forefathers created the custom of bowing in the temple for the simple reason that bowing in a temple provides an opportunity to turn within and experientially gain knowledge of who we truly are. In this way, the temple can serve as a mirror for seekers. After the cleansing and clarity the temple provides, whatever work we do and decisions we make will be beneficial for everyone.

In fact, this is the reason so many temples have been built: so that in the midst of the din and roar of the marketplace everyone can be reminded of peace and patience.

Furthermore, this belief prevents people from considering a temple to be "just another building". Following rituals emphasizes the importance of the temple and the spiritual activity within it.

However, today people have forgotten the actual purpose, and bowing down before a temple has become a mere ritual. If they forget to follow this ritual, their mind becomes anxious. The true message is lost. Temples were meant to decrease one's anxiety, not to increase it.

 **Myths**

12. At least on the day of a festival — for example, the festival of Holi — people should not fight with each other.

 **Reality**

When wise people created this belief centuries ago there was a deeper understanding behind it. The goal was to enable everyone to experience love and harmony with others for at least one day. Some people fight all year round. If such people could stop fighting for at least a day — if they could taste love and harmony for even this short span of time — then perhaps they would keep themselves away from arguments all year round.

Revelation

Festivals were originally introduced so that a person could adopt a resolution and adhere to it for at least one day. When people receive positive results, then they gain conviction that it's possible to live out their resolutions for a day. And if it's possible for that length of time, there's hope that it is possible for longer periods as well.

So, why wait for a festival? Practice taking on daily resolutions. You can vow to speak mildly for one whole day. You may decide to devote yourself to making others happy for one day.

Myths

13. Wearing black clothing is inauspicious.

Today it's widely known that different colors interact with light differently. The color white, for example, reflects light. This attribute produces a cooling effect when you wear it or view it. Because white reflects more light than other colors, many spiritual beliefs grew around it. White became the symbol of purity of mind.

On the other hand, the color black absorbs light instead of reflecting it, and so it became the symbol of darkness (keep in mind, this too is a belief). Black also affects the body differently in different climatic conditions. As a result of this, some people consider black as good, while others believe it to be bad.

Even if the color black is, as the belief says, inauspicious, it's unreasonable to assume it to be inauspicious for everyone. The decision to wear black is a personal choice. If you don't want to wear it, don't. But don't be afraid of it out of a blind faith; avoid it because of a basic understanding of the color.

Revelation

Some religions have associated black with the forces of evil. Other religions have considered black to be auspicious. In some spiritual practices, it's actually recommended to wear black for better meditation, as it's said to help an individual to go within smoothly.

In the long run, the color of your clothes doesn't matter when compared to the thoughts you entertain. Once your understanding of the truth increases, you'll be able to go beyond all worries and concerns about colors.

 Myths

14. Houses should face the direction recommended by Vastu- Shashtra (a Hindu tradition of space design to promote harmony with natural forces, similar to the Chinese tradition of Fengshui.)

Environmental energy, as this type of placement is categorized, has only a small effect on your life. The thoughts that you keep are far more important than the direction your house is facing. This belief leads to constant worry that something bad will happen. After all, a man thinks, his house is facing in the wrong direction. That's only the first step in the destructive progression of this belief. Soon anything bad that happens in his life is attributed to the unfortunate placement of his house. If only it would stop there; but it doesn't. Once this way of thinking grabs him, it's as if it rules his life. It's not illogical to expect him to eventually get trapped in this vicious cycle of negative thought. In the long run, it may

even bring about his downfall. *This is where you must be cautious in your thinking. You can try improving environmental energy, but don't take it to extremes. If you are not able to change the direction of your house, that's fine. Change the direction of your thoughts instead.*

Revelation

Imagine a marketplace with shops facing in different directions; some are even facing each other. All of the shops are making money. The entire market place, in fact, is crowded. Even the stores facing in the allegedly wrong direction seem to be prospering.

How can that be? It's possible because all the shop owners have the right mindset, and that means all directions provide good fortune. When all of the owners are receptive to positivity they all thrive, regardless of the direction their storefronts are facing.

Until your basic thought pattern changes and you become receptive towards positivity, these beliefs may exert an influence over you. Man will change the direction of his house, or wear a good luck charm, hoping that something good will happen. All these small exercises may help him improve his mindset. It's far more likely, though, that he'll eventually become a slave to them. If one sees from the angle of freedom, then it's a big price to pay for a little peace of mind.

Our thoughts have by far the biggest effect on our lives. They can end all doubts. If we change our thoughts, everything else will fall into place.

 **Myths**

15. A dip in the great river Ganges (or any other holy river) washes away all sins and previous wrongdoings.

Reality

A person harbors feelings of guilt due to his previous wrongdoings. His thoughts of remorse reprimand him more than the actual punishment itself. He cannot live and enjoy life fully. The burden of repentance prevents him from living in the present. This in turn adversely affects his deeds in the present.

The custom of taking a dip in the river Ganges was invented to allow people to liberate themselves from this ill feeling. They can seek forgiveness and start leading a completely new, righteous life. They also resolve not to commit such sins in the future.

Revelation

As you gain understanding about the ultimate truth, simply by listening to and contemplating on it, you can rid yourself of previous wrongdoings. When you gain understanding about what virtuous deeds and sins are, who you truly are, and how things are happening spontaneously, then you rid yourself of the feeling of "doer-ship". This helps you release yourself from the guilt of your sins, as well as from the pride of your virtuous deeds. You can then help to spread this higher understanding and awakening to people around you.

■ ■ ■

13
Myths about Prayer

J ust as myths swirl around the topics of God and spirituality, there are many false beliefs when it comes to prayers.

Myths

1. Prayers should be long and studded with special words and Sanskrit chants.

 **Reality**

Prayer is not the Sanskrit shloka, the Arabic aayat, nor the Christian chant. Prayer is a wordless call to the Almighty. Prayer is the feeling of the heart. Words formed by the intellect are only obstacles to true prayer. When the intellect is sacrificed, then the call from the heart emerges.

Prayer is the thirst for the Lord; the feeling of gratitude toward the Supreme Being. When the mind is turned within it is fearless. Only a fearless mind prays for the well-being of all.

 **Revelation**

Picture an individual who gave a million dollars to charity. You might think this action will bear great fruit. That could very well be true. The ultimate deciding factor, though, is the intent with which it was given.

The truth of the matter is that nothing may come of the gift if his feeling is less than charitable. If he is being compelled to donate only to appear generous in the eyes of people, then his act of donation will not bear fruit. Why? Because this person's motive is not pure. He is donating reluctantly for the sake of his image. There is a feeling of compulsion — not compassion — behind his deed.

Picture another person who gives only ten dollars to charity. In contrast, the motivation and feeling with which he gives this money is of great significance. He thinks, "I wish I had more money to give. More people could have benefited. Even so, I hope these ten dollars can be of some use at least." This donation, however small, will bear great fruit.

There once was a farmer who prayed daily without fail. He recited a different prayer every day by reading it from a book. Not a single day did he miss his prayer. One day he was travelling to the city. On the way he remembered to pray, but he had forgotten to take his book along. So he prayed, "O Lord, my memory is poor, but you know all my prayers. I will slowly say the alphabet (A, B, C, D…) three times. Please compose a prayer out of these." He then recited the alphabet. God said to His angel, "Many different prayers have come to me, but today I have received the best one!"

However impressive an action may appear, it is useless if the feeling or intention behind it is less than altruistic. If the act is performed out of guilt, then it is the guilty feeling that bears the fruit, and not the action. It's not the size of the gift that provides the blessing, but the intention behind the gift. The most celebrated acts, or those acts which appear admirable to others, do not necessarily reap good results.

You need to understand that karma (actions), in and of itself, does not bring results. In truth it is the feeling or intention behind karma that actually brings results. The feelings behind your prayer are the important part; activate them and enhance them.

 Myths

2.   Prayer must be performed in a special time, place, and environment.

🔍 Reality

You can pray at any time, in any place, using any posture. Before you pray, though, you'll want to prepare your mind. This habit is especially useful when you're beginning your spiritual journey. As with actions, it's the feelings behind the prayer that make the largest impact.

The same holds true with rendering service. Regardless of the type of service, it's the feeling or intention underlying it that determines its effectiveness.

Even so, one cannot help but bring politeness to his words or humbleness to his posture and body language when performing service. These attitudes are important, as they help one create the necessary feelings.

Revelation

The essence of prayer is the feeling that is behind it. That's not to say your external actions do not influence the creation of those feelings; in fact, they do. If you are beginning on your spiritual journey, these rituals may be of great help to you. Whether or not you bathe before praying, the results will be the same if your feeling is the same. However, if you bathe before you pray, the action may help to create a clear frame of mind.

Throughout all cultures and all ages, people have created many customs, rites, and rituals with regard to praying. Basically, they all say that you must pray according to a strict set of rules; otherwise your prayers are futile. Remember that it's not the rituals and practices that influence your words to God, but rather the feelings of receptiveness that determine the sincerity of your prayers.

You may have a specific time and place to pray. This is good, because it reminds you to pray. That's not to say you can't pray spontaneously at another time. Any time, place, or posture is appropriate for prayer.

 Myths

3. When you're in trouble God comes to save you in a familiar and expected form.

People pray with a desire to reach out to God and have Him hear them. Therefore, they present Him with pleasing words. Many expect to see

God act in their lives because of these pleasing prayers. God does, indeed, manifest Himself to individuals. Very often, though, this manifestation is missed or misinterpreted. This is because each person possesses his own personal vision or image of exactly what God looks like. Many individuals assume that they'll see God in the same form that He is depicted in movies or television programs like "Ramayana" and "Mahabharata".

Man does a marvelously imaginative job at conjuring up a God that is created in his own image, complete with costume, jewels, and all the trappings befitting a Supreme Being. He then expects that God will wear this guise when He appears before an individual.

Because of this pre-conceived concept, even if God provides him guidance through the actions of another individual, he won't recognize it. He will credit something other than God for this "good fortune".

He may even become angry at God because he can't see the proof of the fulfillment of his prayers in the exact manner that he has imagined it.

Revelation

Once a powerful flood began to engulf an entire village. People bustled about in order to survive the raging waters. They took every possible route of escape. One individual in the village possessed an intense faith in God, so he prayed to God for help. The moment he uttered his petition, several people passed by him swimming in the water carrying a rope. They offered the rope to him as a means of escaping the flood. But he told them, "No, God will rescue me. I have full faith in Him."

The water level rose, and he continued to pray, when a boat approached him. In the vessel were several people escaping from the flood. They called out to him, encouraging him to get into the boat. He, however, was not ready to go. He kept saying, "My God will definitely come to my rescue."

Now the water rose to a dangerous level. He climbed up onto the roof of his house in order to save himself from drowning. A few moments later, some members of the armed services flew over him in a helicopter. They dropped a ladder toward him. Still, he was adamant and refused their help.

"God will save me," he said confidently.

Finally, the man drowned. After his death, he saw God and asked the obvious questions, "Oh God! Why did You allow me to drown and destroy my faith? Why didn't You come to my rescue?"

God replied, "I gave you a rope, a boat and a ladder, but you were not ready to be helped. You wished to see my help according to your own private image. You couldn't recognize me even when I was right in front of you."

 **Myths**

4. You should only ask for the highest things in prayer.

You can ask for anything in prayer. There is nothing wrong with that. An individual may begin with prayer out of greed and desire. The conclusion of prayer, though, must be selflessness.

Consider the parents of a small child who want to teach him virtues. They ask him to share whatever he has with his younger brother. He refuses to listen. He says, "If I give him a part of my share, I will get less."

The father, though, insists, "If you give him a portion of your meal, I'll give you a big piece of chocolate." Now the child is excited. With this enticement, he obeys and he receives his promised piece of chocolate.

In this way, he gradually realizes the happiness of giving. He experiences the pleasure of helping others. As he continues in this learning, the young lad doesn't need any kind of bribe before doing something good. He begins working selflessly.

Revelation

Similarly, in the beginning you may pray for worldly items. Your faith increases when you receive these things. When these smaller results begin to surprise you, you wonder, "Am I going to ask for such minor things all my life? Or are there greater things for which I can pray? Can I ask for the provider Himself in prayer?"

Thus with the power of prayer, anything can be attained. You can also ask for God Himself.

 **Myths**

5. The same prayer has to be repeated every day. You must not change the wording of your prayer.

Prayers need to be revised periodically in order to remain appropriate for changing situations and levels of understanding. Prayer is a powerful medicine. It has a tremendous effect on your body, mind, and intellect. You may not realize this. Everybody prays, but only a few know what should be done while praying. This can be compared with having a prescription for medicine, but being unaware of how much medicine to take or how often it must be taken.

Revelation

A father and his son were praying one evening. The father asked the son,

"What did you ask for?" The son replied, "I said to God that when I grow up, I would like to be just like my father." Upon hearing this, the father changed his prayer: "Oh God! Please make me like what my son believes I am." In the same way, prayers change with every situation based on your level of understanding.

■ ■ ■

14
Myths about Meditation

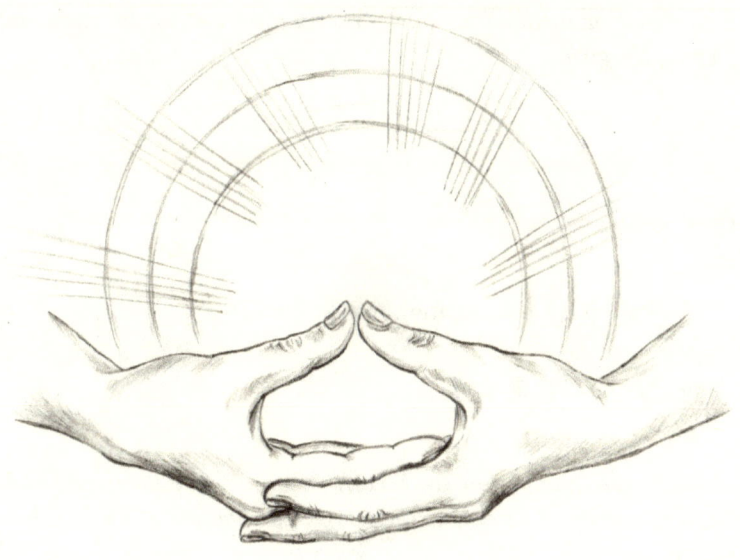

Many people feel intimidated by meditation, visualizing it to be like a monk sitting in lotus posture for hours atop a mountain. They believe that meditation is meant for the recluse, not for householders. Let's unravel some of the myths related to meditation here.

 **Myths**

1. Meditation is concentration.

Reality

Many people practice meditation by focusing on the breath. *This is not meditation; it is a concentration exercise. Concentration signifies focusing the mind on one particular point to the exclusion of everything else. When the mind is full of thoughts, concentration exercises can make it sharp, sensitive, and alert. It is important to understand that concentration is not the goal of meditation, but concentration can be instrumental in achieving the goal.*

 **Myths**

2. Meditation is contemplation or reflection.

Reality

Today the word "meditation" has become commonplace and is used without an understanding of its deeper meaning. "Meditation" is frequently used synonymously with such terms as "reflection" or "contemplation." As a result, its true significance has been lost.

In contemplation we think about a subject from all possible views. We may first think about the positive aspects of that subject and then focus on its negative aspects. Finally, we know about that subject in depth and may understand it fully. Our concentration improves in the process. This, however, is not meditation.

 **Myths**

3. Meditation is relaxation.

 **Reality**

Relaxation techniques, such as Pranayam or Shavasan, help to quiet the body and mind. They prepare the body and mind for meditation. This altered or relaxed state of mind itself, however, is not meditation.

 **Myths**

4. Meditation is intention, or self-control, or willpower exercises.

 **Reality**

The mind is continuously filled with insatiable desires. No sooner does one desire get fulfilled than another arises. By fulfilling these never-ending desires we become slaves of the mind. By following an intention, or using willpower exercises, we can hold back these desires for a limited time. Our self-control increases. Later, it depends on us whether to fulfill a desire or to give it up. Although we can master our mind briefly with such practices, this is not meditation.

 Myths

5. Meditation is attuning the body to energy.

Reality

Some people believe that attuning the body to Kundalini(spinal energy) is meditation. However, rather than dealing with energy, meditation transcends the plane of energy. Meditation is about experiencing the essence of un-manifest existence that is beyond manifest energy.

Myths

6. Meditation means performing austere acts, such as standing on one foot through day and night. The foot swells, but you will not shift from your position.
7. Meditation means penance, like lying on a bed of nails, burying the body under the ground up to the neck, not taking food for prolonged periods, or performing chanting repeatedly.
8. Practicing yoga is meditation.
9. Attaining mystical powers is meditation.

Reality

The word "meditation" originates from spirituality. Historically, spiritual seekers in India understood the deeper aspects of meditation.

They were stabilized in the supreme bliss. They practiced yoga, performed penance, and withstood austerities, to see whether they could remain in the same blissful state even during a changed state of body. However, with the passage of time, meditation became identified with these ritualistic customs and techniques. Such practices gained importance while the actual purpose of meditation became lost. Some people even practiced these techniques to attain mystical powers. However, these techniques are not meditation.

 **Myths**

10. Meditation is a way of escaping from problems.

Reality

We are faced constantly with a profusion of problems that may involve relationships, health, financial issues, conflicts in our neighborhood, difficulties at work, or even issues at the national level. Many people act reactively, by jumping to solutions as soon as such problems arise. They would consider meditating in the midst of such problems an escape from reality; but nothing could be further from the truth. When we meditate we are freed from the clutter of the mind. We become liberated from past beliefs that can influence our approach to present and future problems. As we delve deep into meditation, we reach the state of stillness. Our level of consciousness rises. With higher awareness, we begin to observe problems moving towards resolution on their own. This is a miracle that we need to witness.

 **Myths**

11. Meditation is too difficult. Practicing meditation requires a hard struggle and a lot of effort.

Reality

We do not need to actively do anything in meditation. We just need to sit and do nothing. We only need to witness whatever is going on within, and know the Knower of everything. We do not need to resist anything. Thus, meditation is effortless effort.

 **Myths**

12. Meditation is meant for monks or recluses.

 **Reality**

Many people associate meditation with an image of an ageing hermit seated with closed eyes on some remote mountainside. They believe it is necessary to renounce the material world to meditate, and to progress on the spiritual path. However, meditation is meant for people of all walks of life and all age groups. Everyone can meditate, be they student or businessman, householder or pensioner, man or woman, alone as an individual, or in a group. Meditation can be practiced whether we are in solitude or in the din and roar of the marketplace.

 **Myths**

13. Meditation is meant for retired or older people.

 **Reality**

Meditation is meant for everyone. It is universal. One can practice it from childhood and it will add value to life. Children find their concentration improves with the practice of meditation, and they are able to perform better in class. Teens find meditation helps them to be more focused and goal-oriented in their studies. People are relaxed and more efficient in their workplace with meditation. For the householder, meditation can help attain greater harmony in relationships.

 **Myths**

14. Meditation means sitting for hours in one place with eyes closed.

Reality

The ultimate goal of meditation is to be in a state of love, joy, and peace. This can be while we are seated or walking, sleeping or awake, with our eyes closed or open. However, to begin our meditation practice we sit in one place, with eyes closed, for at least 20 minutes. With consistent practice we may later sit in meditation for a longer time; but this is optional.

 **Myths**

15. "Out of body experience" or astral travelling is meditation.

Reality

Astral projection (or astral travel) is an interpretation of an out-of-body experience (OBE). It assumes the existence of an "astral body" separate from the physical body and capable of travelling outside it. However, all this happens in the realm of the mind. In meditation, both the body and the mind are transcended. Therefore, such experiences are not meditation.

 Myths

16. Meditation is visualizing an image of God.

 **Reality**

Visualizing involves the presence of the mind. So, seeing an image of God is in the realm of the mind. The image of God is specific to different religions. However, just as the Sun is beyond all religions, meditation is beyond the boundaries of all religions. Meditation is universal. True meditation is about experiencing the one who is knowing: the witness, the witnessed, and also the act of witnessing.

 **Myths**

17. Meditation is meant for those who want to attain salvation.

 **Reality**

Meditation can be practiced by each and every one of us. It is like a wish-fulfilling tree. It is up to us how we derive benefit from it. With meditation we can derive external benefits as well as deeper, spiritual benefits like salvation. It can help us to gain health and harmony in our relationships. More deeply, it can also help us to attain true happiness and peace, which is our innate nature.

 Myths

18. Meditation is a means to gain wealth.

 **Reality**

Some people believe that if they meditate they will be certain to attain

wealth, get the perfect job, or pass their examinations. However, it's not so. It is important to understand that meditation will not lead to sudden riches. Unfortunately, some gurus confound people with such misconceptions. There are priests and pundits who preach techniques of increasing income in the name of spirituality. Many people pointlessly become involved with such techniques. There is nothing wrong with gaining wealth and becoming materially successful. However, meditation has nothing directly to do with this. The ability to earn wealth is different in every body-mind mechanism. Meditation may help in enhancing capacity and efficiency at work, but it is not itself a method of getting a good job or becoming rich.

 Myths

19. Meditation is a waste of time.

Reality

Do we consider taking a shower every day to be a waste of time? Surely not. It is the same with meditation. We can consider meditation as a shower we take to cleanse our mind. It is an investment for a better present and a brighter future. It's like watering a plant every day so that it will grow steadily into a big tree. However, we should not meditate with the anticipation of results in the future.

 Myths

20. Meditation is meant to be practiced only in the early morning.

 **Reality**

Some people avoid taking up meditation because they believe the practice *should only take place in the early morning at dawn. They are not used to waking up so early. Early morning is indeed an auspicious time for meditation. The environment is supportive because our stomach is empty and our mind is still. If we meditate at that time, we can go deeper into meditation. However, this time is not mandatory. We can practice meditation at whatever time we get up, before starting our daily activities. It can also be desirable, if possible, to meditate before retiring for the day.*

■ ■ ■

15
Some Myths about the Guru

L et's explore some of the myths related to the concept of a Guru in this chapter.

Myths

1. A guru is a specific individual who guides you.

Reality

Do you know a person whom you consider your Guru? Is such a thing even possible? Can a Guru be a person in a physical body?

No, a body cannot be a Guru. There are many who mistakenly believe this, though. They have been told "this" person — "this" body — is their Guru. They are forbidden to seek help elsewhere. They are not supposed to attend any other discourses except those given by him. If they do, then they are a traitor. Many individuals live their lives fearing this.

Revelation

A body is not a Guru. The Consciousness which manifests in that body is a Guru. The Consciousness within you that is yet to be revealed is the Guru. It is that Consciousness that guides you. It may guide you through a person, a book, or dream. It can manifest in the form of an external person. So what do you have to do? Just be open and receptive. Don't close yourself, saying that if others can attain Self-realization on their own, then I can too. That's not in your hands. Just be open and let the Consciousness guide you.

Myths

2. A Guru is a teacher. That means any teacher can be considered a Guru.

Reality

A teacher is someone from whom you learn lessons. This means anyone may be your teacher depending on the lessons you need to learn. In fact, anything can teach you a lesson, even the smallest moments of your life.

But the Guru is one who teaches you the final lesson, the ultimate lesson of life. The Guru will stabilize you in the truth. If you do not learn the final lesson, then you will continue to view yourself as a body.

It is from the Guru that you receive this final lesson of "Who Am I?" He establishes you in the truth. You will learn that knowing yourself and knowing God is the same. Self-realization and Godrealization are the same. The Guru imparts that understanding.

Revelation

The teacher provides you with information. You may ask who receives this information. It is your mind. So, the one who gives information about the world to the mind is referred to as the teacher.

But the one who gives information about the existence of the mind — where the mind becomes an object — is the Guru. In essence, the Guru tells you what is beyond the mind.

The purpose of many teachings is to make you successful in the world. The Guru's teachings are meant to establish you in your experience — the experience of Truth — so that your problems dissolve altogether, with no need to solve them one by one.

A teacher gives you information much as a postman provides you with mail. He offers many letters filled with information. The Guru too gives you a letter: a letter bomb. Open it and the bomb explodes to kill the individual — or in other words, the ego — the one who thinks of himself as separate.

Myths

3. A Guru is not required for spiritual growth.

Reality

Is a Guru required? One may as well ask, is mother required? The answer to both the questions is the same.

There are some children who grow up without mothers. Their mothers died at their birth or at some other time during their formative years. Yet they grow; they live. They appear just fine without a mother.

Similarly, there are a few individuals who didn't have a Guru and yet have attained realization; for example, Guru Nanak, Ramana Maharshi, and Gautama Buddha. While they had masters in their lives, they attained realization on their own.

These individuals represent the exceptions. In most cases a Guru is required. Saint Tukaram, Saint Dnyaneshwar, Saint Eknath, Saint Kabir, and many others belong to a long list who had Gurus. The reason is that for the Truth to manifest the mind has to fall, or step aside. The mind can't do this by itself. It is necessary to have faith in someone or something else.

Revelation

Five kings came across a beautiful piece of land in a faraway country. Each of them acquired a part of it and commissioned a palace. They already had palaces to call home, but they built these new palaces, one near the other, so that they could visit them once in a while.

Once the palaces were built, each king asked his eldest son to go and have a look. One of the princes didn't go, saying it was unnecessary. The other four embarked on their journey.

When they met each other along the way they began talking about their palaces. As happens in conversations, one thing led to another. Soon they were arguing about whose palace would be the best. Each gave logical reasons for his opinions.

One reasoned that his kingdom was the richest, so his palace would be the most exquisite. One of them argued that his kingdom had the most skilled artisans of all, so of course his would be the most spectacular. This went on until they reached their palaces.

All of them stopped to marvel at the doors. Standing at the doorstep, they continued their argument based on only the architecture of the doors. If one pointed out that the teak used in his door was supreme, the other sang praises of the magnificent carvings on his door. If one raved about how secure his door was, the other started counting the flaws in the doors of the rest.

While all this was occurring, one of the princes opened the door and walked in. The other three continued their debate. As night fell, they continued their argument, sleeping on the doorstep only to awaken in the following morning and start all over again.

They had been sent there for only a day or two. The arguing continued. They didn't stop even when they had to return home. But the prince who had entered his palace came out in a state of sheer bliss. He returned home ecstatic; he had accomplished the purpose for which he had gone. The other three returned home feeling miserable because they had wasted their time quarrelling with each other.

So what does this parable have to do with a Guru? The prince who stayed home — the one who refused to embark on the journey — is akin to those who say that no Guru is required.

The others reached the palace. The palace represents the aim of all spirituality. You can call the palace by whatever name with which you feel comfortable: God, Enlightenment, or Realization. In the story, the door is also a central feature. The door is representative of the Guru.

Those princes who actually reached the doorstep —that is, the Guru — started arguing about their Guru, their religion, and their portrayal of God. Most of them stayed just at the doorstep, never even using the door. If only they had entered through the door, they would have gone into the palace. But since they didn't, they never learned the Truth. In the story, only one prince was bestowed with the Grace to go beyond the Guru and experience God.

■ ■ ■

16
Myths about Self-realization

For many individuals the concept of Self-realization is difficult to grasp. When people begin to describe it, it seems impossible for mere mortals to attain. We seem to get mired in a host of preconceived ideas about how Self-realized people act, what they wear, how they treat others, and basically how they live their lives in general.

These myths only perpetuate the idea that Self-realization is confined to a very few especially-selected ones, or the very lucky. It's unfortunate so many believe this. Considering the following myths may help you reconsider how a Self-realized person truly acts, and why.

 **Myths**

1. The one who is Self-realized will always experience happiness, and will never be unhappy.

 **Reality**

When one goes beyond the happiness and unhappiness the world offers, the state of Self-realization is attained by his body. One need not force himself to believe it, or employ some clever technique in order to attain that state. Attainment is done through understanding. You can only acquire this understanding by listening to discourses on the Truth. By listening to such discourses, one experientially understands "Who Am I?" and "Why Am I here?" Self-realization, in effect, means transcending happiness and unhappiness; experiencing the state of eternal, unremitting bliss, and being firmly grounded in this state.

 Revelation

After attaining a state of true, eternal bliss, one does not depend on the external, material things of this world for happiness. The happiness derived from pursuing external things diminishes with time. However, the happiness that you derive from acquiring understanding of the supreme truth increases with time. Worldly happiness is attained by pursuing worldly things. However, timeless, eternal bliss can be achieved simply by being who we truly are.

 Myths

2. Self-realization is possible for only a select few.

 **Reality**

If you believe this, you must understand right now that you are holding onto a mistaken belief. This misconception is common, but the true fact is that anyone can attain Self-realization. Whether you are a Hindu or a Muslim, a Christian or a Jew, or a believer of any other religion, it is available to you. You can attain this state of eternal bliss irrespective of whether you are fat or thin, black or white, rich or poor, male or female.

Revelation

The Supreme Consciousness is capable of manifesting in every human being. That is the grace of being born as a human. Animals cannot attain Self-realization.

 Myths

3. Self-realization can give you lots of benefits.

 **Reality**

After Self-realization you transcend worldly gain and loss. We judge everything in the material world by a yardstick of gain and loss. However, through the understanding of the supreme truth, the judging mind itself gets annihilated.

Revelation

The contrasting, comparing mind judges everything. After every incident it evaluates what has just happened. It comments whether it was good or bad, if it caused any gain or benefit. A transaction which resulted in a profit is judged as good or desirable. One in which you experienced a financial loss is deemed undesirable.

Your goal on your spiritual quest is to rid yourself of this judgmental mind. As the judgmental mind vanishes, you will discover eternal bliss within yourself. When the mind starts listening to a series of discourses on the supreme truth it thinks that it will gain something in return. Initially it compares them: whether the earlier discourse was better than the current one.

However, as you continue to listen to the supreme truth, you develop a deeper understanding. You realize that the labels of gain and loss belong to the realm of the mind. When you listen to the truth by putting aside these labels, you get stabilized in the supreme truth. In this way, as you get rid of your judging mind, you go beyond gain and loss.

 Myths

4. The mind can liberate the mind.

The mind really wants to liberate the mind. The mind, though, needs to understand that the only requirement for this action is for it to do

nothing. It only has to keep quiet.

Merely possessing the desire to free the mind also makes the mind stronger. The only help asked of the mind is, paradoxically, to render no help at all. It automatically surrenders itself only through understanding the supreme truth. This understanding is enough to be freed from the contrasting or judgmental mind.

Revelation

As the understanding of the supreme truth takes root in you, your life will indeed become smoother and more natural. The contrasting mind, the one that continually judges all your actions, eventually collapses with this understanding. You need not push it or pull it this way or that; it will require no effort on your part. The instinctive mind works regardless of what you do throughout the day.

This may seem counter-intuitive at first. When some people first hear that the contrasting mind must fall, they begin to work at making it fall. They put much effort into this act. They are then surprised when all this work doesn't result in the death of the mind. They are even more surprised to discover that the mind, through all this work, only grows stronger by the day.

In this state of "understanding", the mind is compelled to listen to the Truth regardless of whether it approves of or likes it. It actually would prefer to work according to its own whims.

That's exactly why you're warned, "Don't bring your mind when you come to listen to the Truth. Leave it outside of the room, just as you leave your shoes outside." This means that you are advised to also leave your prejudices, preconceived notions, previous knowledge, and labels.

 Myths

5. For you to experience Self-realization you first need to perform much penance and put in much time. It takes seven lifetimes.

 **Reality**

The only criterion to achieve Self-realization is the possession of a "label-

free mind". This means you don't need to perform any type of penance. Think about a new born baby. The infant exists label-free and Self-realized. It's only as he engages in the world, with his parents, teachers, and relatives that he begins to respond to the labels the outside world assigns him. The first label he receives is a name. That's only one of a long list of labels the world attaches to him. Many more labels are assigned, viz:

The label of name: I am Tom, I am Harry…

The label of religion: I am Hindu, I am Muslim, I am Sikh, I am Christian…

The label of relation: I am a brother, I am a sister, I am an uncle, I am an aunt…

The label of profession: I am a doctor, I am an engineer, I am a businessman, I am a watchman, I am a shopkeeper, I am a professor…

The body-mind label: I am a man, I am a woman, I am a friend, I am an enemy, I am a householder, I am a monk, I am a fool, I am intelligent…

Revelation

These are only a few of the many labels that are strapped to us every day. It's because of these labels that we live outside our true state of eternal bliss. To get rid of all these labels, we must have a true Guru in our lives. Until the Guru enlightens us about these labels, we cannot break free from them. It's only when these labels fall aside that we can remain in the state of true eternal bliss.

These beliefs deceive you into thinking that you are something else. As these beliefs are cast off, the state of Self-realization is revealed. Then it becomes easy to know, "Who am I?"

Your belief "I am the body" is the strongest label you'll have to address. The body through which you speak is what you believe to be "you". Actually, the body is only the door through which we speak; it is just an instrument.

A baby comes into the world through its parents; they are essential for the baby's birth. It can be said that the parents are "the door" through which the baby enters the world. But then the parents begin to think as if their child is their possession. So it is with your body. It's only a medium through which you come to know the true Self, the universal Self.

Someone who has lost one or more of his limbs in an accident feels complete from within. He doesn't become a partial person, even when a limb has been severed. The feeling of being, which is present in each and every one of us, is always complete.

But yet, we continue to believe "I am the body". The body is a non-living object just like a fan or a table. It may take you a while to come to terms with this idea. But to live with the belief that the body is the real "I", or "I am separate", is called ego.

We have such strong identification with our bodies, and believe them to be the one we are, that even if someone points out that we are not the body we don't believe him immediately. But we have to accept the truth that the one we truly are and the body are two different things.

Consider the example of a microphone. A microphone is just an instrument through which a person speaks. The person says, "I am speaking." As the words emanate from the mike, the mike believes that it is speaking. This is an illusion.

If you were able to speak to the mike, you would say, "Hey! You're just an object. The one who is speaking through you is the real speaker, the Subject. You may call it Consciousness, the Self or God."

Your spiritual goal is to speak through the body, knowing Him. This is the ultimate goal of human life. Knowing Him means knowing our true Self. That's the very moment we come to know that the body is just an instrument, and we then allow it to work just as an instrument.

When you achieve Self-realization you gain conviction that "I am not the body." The "I" was there before the body, and the "I" will be there after the body is gone. Even right now, if you close your eyes and meditate on your being, on the "I am" feeling, you'll notice the changes occurring involve only body and not your "Being."

As a child, your being (the feeling that "I am") was the same as it is now. Even when you close your eyes and imagine you are old, the feeling of your being will remain unchanged, as it is now. When you speak with older individuals, they inevitably say they feel no differently than when they were 20 years or younger. Why? Because their "Being" is unchanged, regardless of their age. Once you understand this incredible concept, you'll finally understand that all changes— be they happiness, sadness, pain, stress, or aging — are merely on the body level.

While you may believe we've talked about all the different labels society places on us, there's one more we've yet to discuss. This is "I am the mind." For some, this is just as difficult a label to shake. The mind, though, is just a bundle of thoughts. We tend to be happy or sad based on how we're thinking at that particular time.

Actually, your thoughts of happiness or sadness are really the only things which keep changing. Your thoughts are so firmly glued to you that you live your entire life believing yourself to be actually these thoughts.

On any given day, at any given time, you may have a flurry of various thoughts, like "I am sad." Does it ever occur to you to actually ask, "Who is sad"? The truth is that this is a thought — that's all. As this particular thought enters the mind, why do we leave our center, or defocus from our heart, to become one with the thought? We are, in effect, only forgetting who we are.

This can evolve into a less than ideal situation. A thought may enter your mind and you may adopt it. You may stick to the thought. "I am getting bored," is another example of a thought. As you think it, you may begin to believe you are really getting bored.

When you identify yourself with your thoughts you become something that's not your real Self. You become these false ideas. To believe you and your thoughts are one is probably the largest illusion you hold.

This is why breaking this belief is absolutely necessary for the final understanding to manifest. Following this manifestation, your thoughts will be nothing more than a medium for you to experience yourself. This means that at night when you're in deep sleep no thoughts exist, and there is no experience of the Self.

It is, without a doubt, difficult for the novice spiritual seeker to understand that the body and the mind are only media. You can compare this to carrying a mirror wherever you go. No matter where you go, you see your Self, you feel yourself.

Sometimes the mirror you're holding is full of thoughts; sometimes you're holding a mirror of pain. Ultimately, though, when you attain Self-realization it doesn't matter. It doesn't change your true feeling of "I am." What would happen if tomorrow this mirror broke? Nothing. Nothing at all. You would still be as "I am."

Remember that when you're in the deep sleep we mentioned earlier, there are no thoughts, and that means you're not able experience the Self. But even then "I am" is still there, because you wake up in the morning and say, "I had a good night's sleep." But who really is saying this? He who was there in deep sleep is there even now. Knowing Him (the real I) is Self-realization.

When these two labels, that of the body and the mind, are eliminated, then you (the one who has the feeling of being a separate entity) fall away. The mind drops. This individual, whose origins are in thoughts, finally receives the understanding that it is merely a thought. Letting go off the individual is termed Self-realization.

Myths

6. I will be realized one day. An individual gets realized.
7. I can and will realize myself independently of any help from others.

Reality

Again, this is a popularly held belief with no basis in fact. In reality, it is the Self that realizes itself. An individual has never been Self-realized. Remember that the individual must fall aside for any Self-realization to occur. You may say that Ramana Maharishi attained realization, Guru Nanak got realization, Mahavir and the Buddha got realization. But you would be misspeaking. No individual has ever attained Self-realization.

Revelation

The individual — that is, the one who thinks he is separate — drops away. It has to be. It can be no other way. It's this falling away that brings about Self-realization. How else would an individual become Self-realized?

When you believe that "I am my thoughts" it only makes the individual stronger. As true understanding comes through, then it is understood that there never was an individual. The mind is a slave of appreciation: when someone appreciates it, it becomes happy; when someone insults it, it becomes unhappy. When this mind — which weighs everything within the realm of good or bad — drops away, the experience of being, or Selfrealization, then manifests.

Myths

8. When the individual falls away and Self-realization occurs, you'll see an amazing transformation in one's outward actions. For example, the Self-realized individual will stop eating non-vegetarian food.

Reality

This belief is not only one of the most popular myths concerning this topic, it's also one of the largest hurdles along the path of Selfrealization. Throughout history, without exception, all realized souls have had the same experience; but their expressions of the truth were different. These persons adapted this experience as a natural expression of their own manners.

You no doubt know of realized persons who became silent. Others, who spoke little prior to their transformation, began talking more. Others, who never sang prior to Self-realization, started singing hymns. In some cases, illiterate persons began to speak the language of the Upanishadas and the Vedas. Ramana Maharishi went silent for 15 years. The Prophet

Mohammed, who never once thought that he would become a messiah, created the entire Koran.

It's also just as likely that those who attain this state of "understanding" will continue to do what they've always done. The shopkeepers will continue being shopkeepers. The butcher won't stop butchering goats.

A change in the habits, preferences, actions, or even the persona of the person may not occur following Self-realization. Remember that the world judges by appearances. If there is no change in your outward actions and the world looks at you and says, "You are not serene or at peace with yourself," how does it matter? As long as you are serene that's the only concern.

By contrast, if you're not at peace with yourself, but the world views you as being at peace, does that really make it so? To what will you give more importance, your own feeling or that of the world?

Revelation

People naturally judge and compare based on outside appearances. They feel the behavior of today's realized beings has to match the legends of those throughout history. But the Self or God or Nature never repeats the same thing: it is always expressed in new ways. Think of the Buddha, Meera, Ramana Maharishi, Mahavir, Kabir, Tukaram, Eknath, Namdev, Guru Nanak, and Jesus, to name just a few who expressed themselves in different ways.

It's the unrealized human mind which insists a realized person must walk in a particular way or talk in a certain way. When the person's actions don't comply with this stereotypical image, then the mind concludes that he or she is not realized. The mind sees everything in a fixed pattern and a very specific way.

The mind does this so it won't have difficulty in understanding. The mind wants to fix everything. This need to establish patterns and create preconceived notions is in fact a large hurdle to Self-realization.

 **Myths**

9. After Self-realization you'll never get angry. Your eyes will always be full of love.

 **Reality**

Once again we encounter an idea with no basis in fact. Of course you're going to get angry. Knowing that, your next logical step would be to assume you'll feel remorseful following an outburst of anger. You may very well believe the Self-realized person quickly reviews his actions and says to himself, "I got angry and I really shouldn't have. I'll do better the next time."

Revelation

You may think this, but even this is a false belief. For the person who is Self-realized the only reaction that's available, from his viewpoint, is that of witnessing or understanding.

In every event — even one involving anger —there is only witnessing. A person merely observes what happens through his body-mind, be it love or anger. When in solitude, he doesn't think, "Nowadays, I don't get angry…I am polite…I sit this way… I walk that way..."

You'll find there are many individuals who don't get angry at all. Does this mean they are all Self-realized? There are many who remain calm regardless of the situations in which they find themselves. Do they all possess the ultimate wisdom? Additionally, there are actors who play the role of not getting angry. Does that mean that all of them are wise?

Myths

10. The Self-realized don't dream.

 **Reality**

Once you experience Self-realization all you see is "the dream." Not only will you dream at night, but you'll actually see the dream during your waking hours as well. You'll recognize that life is a dream. Because of this, you'll become a witness — an observer — to all sorts of scenes. Before Self-realization, you watch this scene play out and consider this all to be real; you consider it to be the truth. You witness the same events and participate in the same scenes believing everything to be true. When you attain Self-realization, any action, any experience, or anything that's apart from God is only a dream or an illusion.

 Revelation

The statement that those who are Self-realized see nothing but a dream can be understood through the following example. You're watching a movie in a theater. At one point, a fire erupts "on screen" that is a part of the story line of the movie. That fire, though, doesn't destroy the screen. That fire is not "real" in the sense that it's occurring in the theater itself. The screen isn't burnt, nor does the fire spread beyond the screen into the audience. In much the same way, all changes life produces are only scenes of a movie; they can't hurt the screen. The changes of life don't injure the Witness, who is you when you're Self-realized.

 **Myths**

11. Renouncing the material world is absolutely necessary in order to

attain Self-realization. After a person experiences Self-realization, he renounces everything.

Reality

Upon achieving Self-realization, the act of renouncing is in itself actually renounced. In other words, the very act of renouncing doesn't make a difference if you're Self-realized.

Revelation

Remember the admonition to be neither a recluse living in the forest nor a householder mired in the miseries of daily life. Instead, you'll discover you'll be what's called a "Bright Householder." This is a person who lives beyond both of those extremes.

The recluse runs away from life. He's always giving up one thing or another... or more than likely, everything. Many believe this is the path to Self-realization, as well as the path the Self-realized walk. But the truth is there's only one thing you must give up, and that's the idea of giving up.

At the other extreme is the householder, the family man (or woman), the one whose world revolves around his family. The realized one doesn't live at this end of the spectrum, either. As a "Bright Householder," he understands that it's useless to run into the forest for the purpose of getting away. But he's also well aware that there's no use in hiding behind the cover of his family, either.

Where does he walk, then? He travels the middle path between these two choices, and he's confident that this is the proper path for him. This means he's fully living in this world and carrying out all the responsibilities of daily life. His life differs from others because all of his activities are aligned to the attainment and expression of the supreme truth.

Myths

12. A realized person will always be in the state of Samadhi (timeless state of meditation), or a state of deep meditation.

Reality

As being in the experience of the Self becomes effortless for a realized person, he comes to know that Samadhi is his nature. This means he doesn't need to sit in one place and meditate. When "being" becomes effortless, then Samadhi starts bearing fruit. The instinctive mind presides over all activities. The body's role, or the purpose or goal for which it's on the earth, then begins. Self-expression naturally follows Self-realization.

Revelation

Samadhi doesn't require a person delve into a deep meditative state, as many believe. It can be experienced in the waking state. But more than that, once you've attained Self-realization you'll see there really is no need to bring that experience to the waking state; it's already there. You've just been unable to experience it before because your imagination and mind have been doing what they've wanted to up until now. The mind, you may recall, captures an experience or a thought and then passes judgment on that experience.

Among other thoughts, it thinks, "In deep sleep, the feeling of the body disappears; pain and suffering are not felt. The same state should be attained in the waking state." When you make the effort, though, to attain that state when awake, the mind then complains, "Oh! The feeling of the body is still there. My head is throbbing. My back is aching from sitting in one place for so long. I can't feel this experience even though it's present in deep sleep. If the Experience of Being is continuously going on, why am I not able to experience it?" This is not subtle. But if you actually perceive this, it's felt to be very subtle, as well as very difficult to grasp.

 **Myths**

13. Once a person attains Self-realization he begins to preach and spread wisdom.

 **Reality**

This, again, is what many expect people to do once they reach this summit. They also believe that when they reach this point themselves, they'll be compelled to do it. Rest assured; there is no rule, written or unwritten, which requires the spreading of wisdom.

Experience seems to predict that in the majority of cases the Truth has been spread by those individuals and shared with all. Guru Nanak moved around and shared his knowledge with everyone. Meera danced and sang hymns and spread her devotion among people. Though there's only one Truth, people have spread and expressed it in their own unique style.

 Revelation

You may not be aware that there have been many who have attained realization but remained quiet throughout their lives, continued doing their usual jobs, and passed away unnoticed.

 Myths

14. You receive an experience of energy, or smell a certain fragrance, if you go near a person who has achieved realization.

Reality

This myth, too, is unfounded. You may begin to understand this better when you realize that individuals existed who disliked Lord Buddha, Jesus, or Meera. Some of these individuals even went so far as to hurl stones at them or crucify them. If these truly Self-realized persons actually emanated an energy or fragrance, why didn't their enemies experience it?

Revelation

Granted, some experiences arise because of the strength of the faith of the individual. When those who have the desire to know the Truth come in contact with a realized person, they really do experience energy, peace, power, bliss, and so on. A non-believer, though — an egotistical person — is not receptive to this. He does not then experience this surge of energy or emanation of fragrance.

Myths

15. Any person who is Self-realized not only is capable of performing miracles, but is required to perform miracles.

Reality

This is another erroneous belief that many individuals stubbornly cling to. It's exactly this thinking that has allowed people to be tricked by those claiming to be realized. It's also because of this belief — even expectation — that many have tried to prove themselves once they have attained this state.

It is true: there were many realized souls who performed miracles. These acts, though, were effortless. Not only that, but while they were performing the miracle, they weren't concerned with the effects their acts had on others. Their bodies, at this point, were nothing more than a channel through which the miracle manifested.

These miracles were in direct correlation to a specific situation, the need at the time, and the kind of people with whom the realized person was interacting. The miracles, moreover, were performed through the person's body.

The real miracle isn't in the act itself. The real miracle is simply to sit by a realized person; especially if you're a seeker of spiritual truth. It is in such a presence that the individual mind begins to fade away, and it absorbs the knowledge the realized mind holds.

Witnessing a miracle doesn't produce the clarity you might think it would. Some masters did, indeed, perform miracles to reach out to the masses. You must remember, though, that when they did this it was what exactly was required at the time. For the most part miraculous acts only leave the majority of people more confused. The use of miracles was directly related to the level of people's depth of understanding at the time.

Revelation

A seeker may acquire some essence of powers, or Siddhi, as he travels on his spiritual journey. This isn't always the case, however. This may be difficult to believe: any power an individual acquires in this journey is actually an obstacle in his path. That is exactly why a seeker should focus his mind only on the ultimate Truth — the supreme goal of being stabilized in the Truth— and continue on his journey without any concern for Siddhi. This, itself, is the ultimate miracle.

 **Myths**

16. A realized person not only doesn't fall ill, but he's also capable of curing the illnesses of others.

 **Reality**

This is a big myth. The body does fall ill, whether it's the body of a Self-realized person or one not on a spiritual path. But there is a difference between the two circumstances. As a realized person, you'll understand that your body may develop an illness, but you haven't.

The illness only affects your body. You're well aware — unlike those who are not as far along on their spiritual journey — that you are not your body. You are different and apart from it. There is an understanding that just as the body became ill prior to your experiencing realization, it will also experience illness after you've achieved realization.

When the body develops illnesses it experiences pain. Before realization, the belief was, "I am ill; I have pain." But after realization, you no longer identify yourself with your body. The bond you had with it is broken. You know that, "The body is in pain or suffering. I am the Knower of it, the witness. I am not ill; I am not unhealthy."

There's also a corollary to this myth that claims all of those who are realized have the ability to heal the illnesses of others. Not only are they capable of doing so, but it's required that they do this. No, it's not necessary that a realized person heal others, even though many have.

Think of all the saints who have healed people merely with their touch. Before they touched these individuals, though, the saints weren't certain that the recipient would be healed. They were performing a simple and normal event. The Christ healed many during His time. There were also some who received His touch and were not healed. This, though, doesn't mean that all realized souls must do the same. If this were the case, many individuals would approach realized ones merely for the sake of getting their bodies healed and receiving relief. When true knowledge is attained all identification with the body breaks, and the person then remains focused on the true Self.

 **Myths**

17. The experience of realization is not the same for all persons.

This is erroneous thinking. Every person who has attained realization on this earth has had the same experience. You can't even argue that some had more of this experience and others received less.

There is only one factor which is different: the Truth as it manifested in them was expressed in different ways.

Even today, some individuals believe that if you sing hymns, you attain a special closeness to God. Others believe that if you practice meditation, you attain a special presence with God.

As you progress along the path of understanding, you discover that realization happens first. After that, the real singing of the hymns emerges. In a similar fashion, realization occurs first, then meditation follows. First the knowing of "Who am I?" occurs, then the revelation of pure and supreme knowledge appears.

As you become more grounded in the experience of the Self, the individual in you automatically breaks out of these wrong patterns. You won't need to fight every single pattern individually. The experience is one, but the sharing, expressing and understanding can be different for each person. That is the beauty of the experience.

 Myths

18. Realization is the awakening of the Kundalini power (inner energy), or seeing the light of a thousand suns.

 **Reality**

If there is a desire to experience mystical visions or bright light within, then it is like searching for the experience of Self on the body. This is the biggest hurdle in Self-realization. Whenever the experience of Self-realization is referred, the mind always attempts to experience the Self in terms of the mind and body. The mind always aspires to know and measure everything on its own terms. The experience of Self is the source of life. It cannot be measured or known by the mind's scale.

Experiences of the mind diminish with time. All the experiences which the mind has come across are fleeting; they exist for a short period of time, and then the mind keeps yearning for them again and again. The experiences that are gained at the level of the body during meditation become an impediment in attaining Self-realization. It cannot be said for certain whether the mind or body will be able to savor the same experience again. Out of ignorance, man may repeatedly long for the same experiences at the body-mind level. Very often, experiences that seem to be gratifying and pleasurable to the mind are major hindrances. The sense of pure presence, of pure awareness, is the ultimate experience. You need not look for any other experience.

Until now, you have believed that "I am bound, I need to attain liberation." However, as your understanding deepens, you realize that you are already liberated. Self-realization is your original nature. Many people believe that one can behold the brightness of a thousand suns after awakening of Kundalini. Such beliefs complicate spirituality, which is actually the simplest.

Be very clear that awakening the Kundalini is only related to the body; it has nothing to do with Self-realization. After stabilization in Self the mind remains unshaken. When the final understanding is imparted, the essential truth of Self-realization is bestowed upon the seeker. The state of Self-realization is already present within you; you only need to realize it through experience.

Revelation

Every night while in deep sleep you're in the experience of "Being" or Self-realization. It is only then the body-mind dichotomy disappears. This world — the mind, the body, everything — melts in the totality. Yet, there is still someone present, someone who experiences this, who never disappears. This is overshadowed by the beliefs of the mind and the body. Just as the clouds hide the sun, the beliefs of the mind hide the truth. If you could just understand this while you were awake, you could effortlessly remain in that state. You could experience the calmness of deep sleep while being awake.

Myths

19. Once you're endowed with the final understanding of the Truth, you leave your religion. Or you must change your religion. Conversion is necessary for realization.

Reality

As you know the Self, in your true nature, you discover the actual meaning of "religion."

Never let go of your religion. This doesn't mean if you are currently a Hindu, you must remain a Hindu; if you're a Muslim, you must remain a Muslim; or if you're a Christian, you must stay with Christianity. Keep in mind that all of these religious names — Hindu, Muslim, Sikh, Christian, Jew, and all other religions — are

only labels society places on a set of beliefs.

You may not have known this until now. But as an infant, you come into this world with a religion of your own. This is referred to as the "Bright religion", which is your true nature. Your true nature, your own religion, cannot be divided. Not only that, but it's the same for all. When you're stabilized in your own "Bright religion" you have reached Self-realization.

Revelation

Society mistakenly refers to communities with similar spiritual beliefs as "religions." But your real religion is unique unto you. The "religion" of water, for example, is to cleanse and soothe. Can it be anything else? Of course not. Contemplate, then, on what your true "religion" is. Consider at length what your true nature is.

Myths

20. After you have attained realization you'll possess the knowledge of the whole world. Once you've attained realization you'll be able to read others' thoughts. You won't need to ask anyone's opinion on anything because you'll know everything.

The mind reads and memorizes books, information, and knowledge of the physical world. The realized person doesn't gain knowledge about the world in that way. He's not interested in reading the thoughts of others. You may notice that when he speaks, many times you may catch glimpses of future events; but that's natural for him. He's not aware as he's speaking that his words will foretell the future in some way. For him, events are all a part of happening.

Revelation

Some people hold the mistaken belief that a realized one will know the past, present and future. The mind, which wants everything to be fixed, also wants to see and know the rules for a Self-realized being. It's difficult for it to understand that realization is a shifting from the mind onto the heart. The heart is more about spontaneity and not about rules.

Myths

21. Once you attain realization you'll no longer go on picnics, watch TV, or even go to the movies. As a realized person you'll only be interested in and talk about knowledge. You'll also change your attire.

 **Reality**

Even after you've achieved realization, the body in which this event has occurred is still attached to its parents, wife, children, friends, and relatives. You certainly don't shun them. The body continues to do everything just as it had been doing up to that point.

Of course you can go out, watch movies, and do everything else just as you did before. There's no one or nothing within to comment on your actions. No one to say, "You are now wise. You should be doing this...you shouldn't be doing that..."

There is, though, a small distinction in your "before" and "after" states. After realization you are actually free from both the desire to watch TV and to not watch TV. There is acceptance of everything, but there is no acceptor.

Revelation

In the lives of the realized there will be laughter, silence, happiness, and astonishment. Like a layman, the realized one may discuss ordinary topics, but also point at "the Truth" within.

The realized one may bargain in the market, but shall also talk to his or her disciples about the bargaining mind (judgmental mind). Whether food is bland or tasty, the Self-realized one shall eat both as offerings to God.

 Myths

22. For Self-realization to occur the body must be purified. The body must be free of all patterns of negativity.

Self-realization means being dis-identified from the body and being stabilized in the true Self. The body, as a mirror, is the medium through which you know your Self. Cleaning this mirror implies removing negativity, breaking the patterns and tendencies of the body, purifying the body-mind, and more.

All this is good, of course, but none of it is mandatory or an essential prerequisite. Shift your focus from the mirror to the one standing in front of the mirror. If you shift from the body to the Self by understanding, then cleaning the mirror throughout your life is not even necessary. The simple act of shifting your attention on the Self will automatically clean the mirror.

Readiness to understand and listen to the truth, as it is, can cause the shifting toward the Self. Being in the Self is your basic nature. It is the core. When realization occurs, body-mind purification automatically follows.

Revelation

First things first. Attain Self-stabilization first. Body-mind purification automatically follows. An enlightened master describes himself as without anger, worry-free, fearless, timeless, and space-less. He also explains that he is in constant meditation. Individuals listen to this and then prescribe what he is describing. They focus on ridding themselves of anger, guilt, worry, and what we may consider the other vices.

But that is really putting the cart before the horse. If you attempt to attain realization this way it'll never work. You're working at it backwards. First you achieve stabilization; the other attributes we normally associate with this state then follow.

 Myths

23. Once you've achieved realization you won't care about anybody. In fact, you'll actually criticize others. You won't care about others getting hurt.
24. After you've achieved realization you won't be afraid of lions, snakes, or other dangerous creatures.

Reality

None of the above statements is necessarily true. If your body-mind mechanism was polite before you achieved realization, there is every reason to believe it will remain that way afterward. When necessary, though, the realized person can and will be aggressive. He has understood that he is neither passive nor aggressive; to consider oneself as either is egoistical. A realized person is neither a good person nor a bad person. He is beyond both good and bad.

As an individual who has achieved, realization you are only a witness to the way in which the body behaves. But in your new-found state, you know that everything is happening through God and by God. Because of this you stop hurting or abusing people.

These misconceptions come into play because the role or job of your body-mind mechanism is to check people's faults. And you will do this. You may use anger, or the pretense of anger, if or when it's required.

The basic survival instinct of the body is to be safe from lions, snakes, and other creatures we deem dangerous. Even after you achieve realization, your body obeys all the laws of nature. It will either fight or flee from a snake or lion when necessary. It will feel hunger, just as it always has. The difference is that you observe all these events from within: the inner experience.

Revelation

Still, many false beliefs regarding Self-realization and a person's subsequent actions persist. Individuals insist on saying that following realization, a person will do this or that, and then cite any number of things. Many con men provide the fuel for these beliefs by pretending to be "god men". It's unreasonable to think that if a person didn't eat bitter gourd before realization, he will start eating it after he attains it.

 ## Myths

25. A realized one will not take care of his health.
26. A realized one will not conduct any business.

Reality

To truly understand why these myths are false, you must understand the heart of experiencing Self-realization. Realized ones are beyond doing and non-doing. They still must have a livelihood. Many of them still must support a family. This, naturally, means they must work at something for a living.

And, of course, they'll take care of their health. You may have read the tales about certain masters, such as Ramana Maharishi or Ramakrishna Parmahansa, who didn't take care of their bodies. This doesn't mean that all others must do the same. Their failure to take proper care of their bodies served a specific purpose. Through their actions, they were able to use their diseases to demonstrate disidentification to their disciples, in the same way as Jesus used His crucifixion. It's only through continued ignorance that people appear to insist all enlightened ones behave in one predictable way. If you understand this, then the path toward enlightenment is easy.

If you don't understand it, then you fall into the trap of believing myths to be true and thinking Self-realization to be impossible. Those who do believe the myths then think, "It can happen to the Buddha but not to me. I don't have the discipline of Mahavir. That means I can't attain the final Truth. I don't have the divine devotion of Meera, so I can't make the necessary progress."

Revelation

Understand first what Self-realization is. Then you shall understand that Self-realization isn't difficult at all.

 **Myths**

27. When a realized one walks, birds chirp, trees dance, and flowers bloom.

These are all actually metaphors. They are not to be taken literally. What these delightful phrases are really telling you is that you will blossom just through contact with an enlightened soul. The beliefs of these persons come to light, then vanish, and in the process they reap the fruit of "Bright happiness." This process has been conveyed by using the analogy of nature.

Revelation

This is the language of poets. They paint the picture of enlightened masters or the Buddha through the eyes and imagination of a poet. The fact of this origin, within the words of a poem, is forgotten, or perhaps never known to begin with. People then start judging the realized ones by their external appearance, hairstyle, beard, language, and politeness.

More con men than anyone cares to admit have created and perpetuated these misconceptions. They dress and act in a typical way that aligns nicely with the myths. By doing so they are able to fool the masses. The time has come to know the truth and bring all beliefs to light.

■ ■ ■

SECTION VI
Demystifying Superstitions

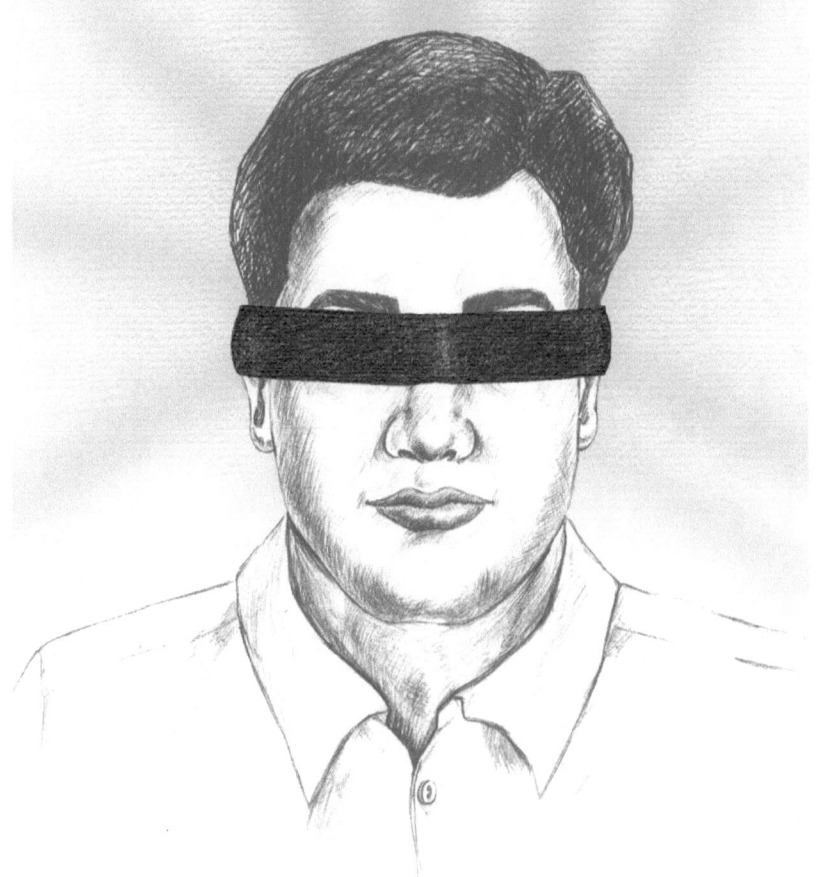

17
An Urban Survey on

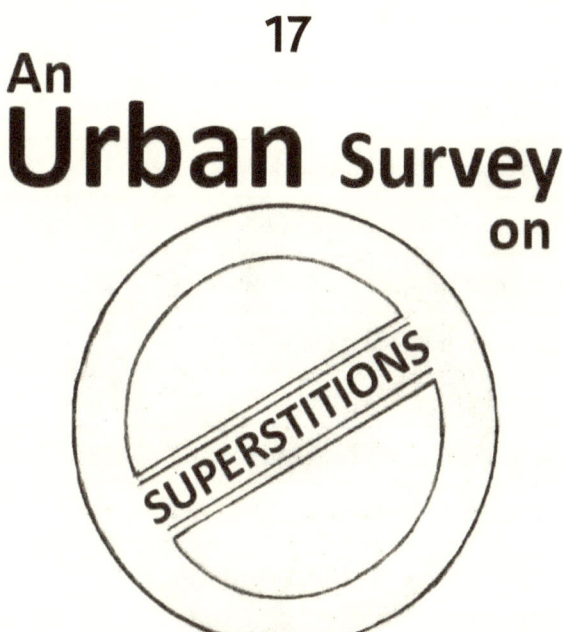

This chapter lists various superstitions prevalent in India. The editors of the book were wondering if such a section is even necessary. The result of a survey carried out by an associated research department, however, convinced us to include this section in the book.

In this survey by Tejgyan Foundation, participants were presented with sixteen statements and were asked to say "Yes" if they believed in the statement and "No" if they didn't. They also had the option to decline to provide any opinion.

Nearly a thousand people from various backgrounds were surveyed from urban India in order to create a sample size that would be an accurate indication of the population as a whole. If the survey were conducted solely in the rural areas of the country, then the results would have been different.

The results of the survey are given below in percentages:

Sr. No.	Belief/Myths	Results		
		Yes	No	No opinion
1.	A cat crossing your path brings bad luck.	30	68	2
2.	God gets angry.	28	71	-
3.	When a lizard falls it's bad luck.	22	78	-
4.	Brooms should not be kept upside down.	35	65	-
5.	Wearing black clothes invites trouble.	27	73	-
6.	Sweeping the house at night is not good.	36	64	-
7.	Girls shouldn't go to a crematorium.	30	70	-
8.	Breaking of a mirror brings bad luck.	28	72	-
9.	If your palms itch, you will get money	31	69	-
10.	A group of three should not undertake any important work.	36	63	1
11.	If your eyes twitch, it is inauspicious.	42	58	-
12.	Howling dogs are a bad omen.	55	45	-
13.	You shouldn't trim nails in the house.	41	59	-
14.	If you laugh more, you will have to cry more.	40	59	1
15.	Shaving the head is essential when there is a death in the family.	55	44	1
16.	If you take salt in your palms, it leads to fights.	20	80	-

The pages that follow expound on some of these myths and many more…

18
Superstitions related to Luck

In the following chapter we'll discuss some of the more widely known superstitions that are thought to bring you bad luck, or in some cases good luck. We'll talk about their origins as well as their relevance.

 **Myths**

1. If you trim your nails in the house then some unfortunate incident will happen to your home. It may get robbed, you may become poor, or other "unlucky" events may occur.

Your nails have no connection with your house being robbed, or any other unfortunate event occurring.

Revelation

This belief probably came about because:

a) There was a possibility of bits of nails getting into food, which could prove to be harmful.

b) The sharp ends of the nails may hurt somebody.

c) Dirt or germs under the nails can potentially spread disease.

 Myths

2. People who have six fingers are considered to be lucky.

Reality

People who have physical deformations are looked down upon, or ridiculed, by some people. This belief began with the self-esteem and wellbeing of those with the extra digit in mind. But this does not mean that they are any luckier than other individuals.

 **Myths**

3. A person with big ears or a broad forehead is intelligent.

Reality

Human beings listen with ears and understand with the brain. Historically, gurus would whisper mantras into the ears of their disciples. For this reason, the ears are considered the doorway to knowledge. Big ears, it is thought by some, indicate that the person knows the "art of listening." This belief also was created, in part, with the idol of Lord Ganesha (the elephant-headed God) in mind. He possesses big ears and a broad forehead and is considered extremely intelligent.

■ ■ ■

19
Superstitions related to People and their Behaviour

The following myths concern people, and their behavior in particular. We'll briefly explain some superstitions, how they originated, and whether they're relevant today.

 **Myths**

1. Don't crack your knuckles.

 Reality

This belief could have originated in several ways:

a) *Cracking knuckles normally communicates a feeling of pain and lethargy. In addition, it spreads that same energy level to those around you. In effect, if you're cracking your knuckles you're spreading pain and laziness to those nearby. It works much the same way that one person's yawning leads to others yawning.*

b) *The habit of cracking knuckles weakens the joints and could eventually cause pain and trembling in the hands later in life.*

 **Myths**

2. You should either cover your mouth or snap your fingers in front of your mouth when yawning.

Reality

Once again, there are noteworthy reasons behind this myth.

a) *When you yawn, there's always a possibility of an insect flying into your mouth. Covering the mouth can prevent this from occurring.*

b) *Yawning is contagious. It only takes one person to yawn in order for others to feel the same need to yawn. By covering your mouth, you can mitigate that contagious effect to some extent.*

 **Myths**

3. If someone is going out somewhere, don't call him from behind or ask him where he is going.

 **Reality**

Calling someone from behind or asking someone where he's going doesn't cause any harmful effects to either him or you.

Revelation

This belief originated when people lived in big extended families. Possible reasons for this superstition are as follows:

a) The individual may be leaving for a specific goal or destination about which he doesn't want other family members to know. If asked, he may feel compelled to lie.

b) If you call to someone and ask where he's going, there is every possibility of others overhearing. If the individual has kept his plans secret from other family members, overhearing may cause discord within the family.

 Myths

4. Don't walk or sleep under a tree in the evening.

Reality

Trees and other plants change their functions during daylight and evening hours. Trees release oxygen in daytime when they conduct photosynthesis, and carbon dioxide at night. Carbon dioxide is harmful for health. Hence, this belief came into practice.

 Myths

5. When you sleep your head should not be facing towards the north direction.

Beliefs which are related to directions are said to have developed because of the gravitational force and magnetic field of the Earth. There must be a proper balance between the magnetic force of the Earth and the magnetic force of your body. This balance is helpful in getting a good night's sleep.

That's why certain beliefs developed regarding the direction in which the kitchen opens, the direction the office door should face, and where the door of the temple should be, as well as the arrangement of other structures and items.

These beliefs can be helpful, but they are not crucial to your wellbeing. What is crucial is to change the thoughts of the person who holds these beliefs. If one's thoughts are positive, then regardless of the direction his head is facing when he sleeps, he can sleep restfully and soundly.

 Myths

6. Three people should not travel together for any important work, or the true goal may not be achieved.

Reality

a) In any important work there may be a need for secrecy. A secret is best kept between two people. When a third individual is involved, there's always the possibility that the secret may inadvertently be revealed. This superstition reduced the chances of a third person getting involved and leaking the secret.

b) Very often, when two people discuss matters the third person feels left out. Because the two of them don't want to hurt the feelings of the third individual, they have to be formal and stilted. They end up discussing irrelevant matters, which only wastes the time of all involved. This belief was invented precisely for this reason.

Myths

7. Don't sit on the threshold of the house in the evening.

Reality

There are two valid reasons for the origin of this myth:

a) When you sit in the doorway, others — adults and children alike — can far too easily trip and fall over you. In effect, you become a safety hazard.

b) The threshold of a door is a dirty area. Dust dropped off from so many pairs of feet passing through tends to collect at this spot. In the evening, when the light is dim, you may not see dust and dirt sticking to your clothes. As a result, you would take it into the house along with you when you return from sitting on the threshold.

20
Superstitions related to Eating Habits

The following myths are all about eating habits. We talk only about the most common, and we know we're leaving out many more.

 **Myths**

1. Before you eat you should sprinkle water around the plate and place a bit of food on the floor.

 **Reality**

These actions bear no consequences to anyone or anything.

Revelation

This superstition was adopted during a period in which people plastered their homes with mud and cow dung. There was no arrangement made to allow light to enter the house, and people used to sit on the floor and eat. This belief was useful in many ways:

a) When the floor around the plate got wet, the probability of insects getting onto the plate and into the food was greatly reduced.

b) Individuals, through the performance of this act, were compelled to wash their hands before the meal.

c) The morsels of food sprinkled on the floor kept the insects busy and the plate safe.

d) The act of eating was viewed as a spiritual practice. Sprinkling water around the plate was a symbolic gesture of thanks giving.

 **Myths**

2. Don't drink milk under the light of the moon. In fact, don't go outside to drink milk.

Reality

This is another belief which originated before the invention of electricity. If something is eaten or drunk in the dark, there is a possibility that insects or contaminants may fall into it unnoticed. You can see how this could be harmful to your health. Milk is commonly drunk before individuals retire for the night. That is why this belief is linked with milk.

Myths

3. Eating curds before leaving the house is auspicious.

Reality

This belief is common in most tropical countries. When you go out, the sudden change in temperature can harm the body. By eating curds, or even drinking a bit of water, you're providing your body some protection from the abrupt fluctuation in temperature.

If the real reason were revealed, there would undoubtedly be an individual or two who would say the rule was created for others and not for him. He would say he's built of a stronger constitution than most people... he certainly isn't affected by such changes in temperature. In order, then, to avoid this line of reasoning, the belief came into existence. The commonly-held belief ensured everyone followed the rule for health reasons. It also served as a method for other family members to remind the individual to eat curds before leaving home.

# Myths

4. A lady should never break a coconut. Only men should break coconuts.

Reality

Nature has made men stronger and women more delicate in build. This is especially true when it comes to the hands of a woman. Her hands are delicate, and the coconut is hard. If a lady tries to break it, the hard surface may injure her. Accept the reality and work accordingly. That's why this superstition sprung up.

Generally, the lady of the house takes care of all the household activities. If guests are expected to visit, then there will be more work. As she's already anxious, she will be more likely to break a coconut in an unsafe manner. Therefore, this belief came into practice for the sake of her safety. Very often this superstition was enforced through the prediction that something bad would befall the lady should she break open the coconut. It's not surprising, then, that many take it as literal fact that it should never be done.

Whether a person is a man or a woman, he or she should take care in breaking anything hard. Furthermore, with the invention of the coconut slicer, coconut breaking has become very convenient. It can be done automatically, easily, and safely, with the press of a button.

■ ■ ■

21

Superstitions Related to Fights

This chapter explores the myths which shroud the topic of fights and arguments: why they were developed, and whether any have relevance to our lives today.

 **Myths**

1. Biting your tongue results in a fight.

Reality

The only time when you could possibly bite your tongue is when you're absorbed in deep thought. At all other times the movements of the tongue and teeth are finely synchronized, so they couldn't possibly hurt each other.

Being in deep thought, however, may produce anxiety, which in turn may lead to arguments. If you find yourself biting your tongue you may want to stay away from other people, rest for some time, and not initiate anything new until you feel less anxious.

 **Myths**

2. When you snap scissors without any good reason — without intentionally cutting fabric or paper — it leads to fights.

Reality

First, let's understand why this belief was originally developed.

a) *We all know that sharp objects can be dangerous. Objects like scissors, key chains, and knives can accidentally break something or unintentionally hurt someone when used carelessly. This myth was created in order to avoid unnecessary damage or injuries.*

b) *Similarly, seeing adults toying with sharp objects can inspire children to do the same. This can be extremely dangerous, especially to their eyes.*

c) *The unnecessary use of a sharp object can reduce the utensil's sharpness and durability.*

d) *The sound of jangling can be irritating, and it may upset other people's peace of mind.*

 **Myths**

3. Playing or toying with door latches or chains causes fights or arguments.

Reality

This belief originated when the doors of houses were not as strong as they are today. Needlessly fooling with the chains could weaken the links, so thieves could break in easily. This belief was created to prevent children from indulging in this habit.

 **Myths**

4. The book Mahabharata should not be kept at home, for it will lead to arguments or disagreements.

Reality

India has always been a very spiritual country. People routinely enjoy discussions concerning spirituality. It's obvious that religious books like the Ramayana, Upanishads, and Vedas are kept at home. But the Mahabharata is an exception to this list. The reasons for this are outlined below:

a) *If a person who is new to the understanding of spirituality reads the Mahabharata with the intention of learning about good conduct,* then he might be misled or confused. In the war epic Mahabharata, Lord Krishna, who is believed to be the complete incarnation of God, is the main character. His words are useful even today. But Lord Krishna employed some unethical methods in the tales of this book. If the reader is ignorant, or a spiritual novice, he may not understand the real meaning behind Lord Krishna's actions. He may then imitate only His actions and fail to practice the deep spiritual path. When people emulate these actions without understanding the reasons behind them, it may prove to be more harmful than useful.

b) The Mahabharata is an epic involving many characters. People may become attached to, or form a relationship of sorts with, their favorite characters. After reading the book, some individuals could also find themselves debating and quarrelling with each other. People may argue over topics such as which characters were subject to curses. Keeping the Mahabharata out of the home prevents this type of behavior.

■ ■ ■

22
Superstitions related to Days and Dates

In this chapter we discuss superstitions and myths surrounding days and dates. Individuals continue to follow some of these concepts without questioning them.

If you find that adhering to these ideas benefits you even today, make use of them. Don't, however, let them become a noose around your neck, restricting your movements unnecessarily.

Myths

1. You shouldn't buy oil on Saturdays.

Reality

At one time people worshipped gods, goddesses, trees, shrubs, the Sun, moon, and stars, and even imaginary objects. Some ceremonies or prayers used to be performed on a grand scale, whereas some would be kept to a minimum. On certain special occasions, people would invite their friends and relatives to their homes.

In those days people employed oil liberally, so much that they used to bathe their entire body in it. As you may guess, after being drenched in so much oil, they would leave footprints of oil on the floor.

When people used to gather on ceremonial occasions, such footprints of oil would increase the chances of people slipping on the floor. This created chaos at times, especially in the presence of children. To avoid accidents, a prohibition was created to stop the use of oil on certain days.

It should be remembered that these guidelines were created with the safety of people in mind. However, as time passed the original purpose of these principles got lost. The guidelines were gradually transformed into superstitions.

Myths

2. The 13 day of any th month is inauspicious.

Reality

This just isn't so. A writer compiled a document of all the bad things that have happened in the world on the 13th of every month. There were quite a few. This made billions of people around the world believe that the date 13 is inauspicious. As a result, many people refuse to venture into any new activity on this date. However, if the same exercise were conducted for any other date, we would find that bad things have happened on all dates without exception. Riots, robbery, murder, crimes and more occur in the world on any given day, 1 through 31; not just on the 13th. Along similar lines, you could easily compile a list of all the good things that have happened on the 13th. You may be surprised to see the quantity of new inventions, openings of universities or colleges, criminals being punished fairly and justly, births of saints, and other wonderful events that have happened on this date.

No date is unlucky or unfortunate. It's only thoughts and wrong beliefs which make it so.

■ ■ ■

23
Superstitions related to Household Articles

This chapter is devoted to demystifying some of the more commonly held superstitions concerning household items.

 **Myths**

1. Don't store your brooms upside down, because something bad will happen.

 Reality

How you store your broom isn't at all related to your ultimate success or failure, or other good or bad events in your life. It's the state of your mind that ultimately brings you success; not the state of the brooms in your house.

Revelation

That doesn't mean that this myth was created haphazardly. In fact, a myth like this could have been developed for good reasons:

a) After sweeping, if a broom is kept upside down, the dust particles stuck to it may drop off and spread around the floor again.

b) The broom handle might get wet or dirty, and when used again it could dirty your hands.

c) If the bristles are pointing upward they may injure someone.

 **Myths**

2. Don't sweep the floor or take out garbage at night.

 Reality

You may have already realized how this superstition began.

a) *Beliefs related to evening and nighttime activities were created before the advent of electricity. Lamps used in those times were dim. This naturally meant it was difficult, if you were sweeping in the dark, to know where the dust would spread. Sweeping is best done during the day to ensure it is performed efficiently.*

b) *Along the same lines, it was best not to empty the garbage at night since it would be hard to see the garbage pile. The possibility always existed of throwing the garbage on some animal, which in turn could attack you.*

c) *Taking out garbage in the dark increased the likelihood that a valuable object would be thrown away.*

 Myths

3. Breaking a mirror brings bad luck.

The purpose of a mirror, of course, is to view your face. For this reason, breaking it is symbolically considered similar to "breaking" an individual.

The real problem, though, lies in the sharp, potentially harmful shards of glass. It's difficult to ensure that every small piece is gathered properly. Even a tiny piece can cause injury. Hence, to be cautious, this belief was developed.

 **Myths**

4. Footwear and brooms should not be kept together.

Reality

A broom is used to sweep and clean the house. The used broom can have remnants of dust and dirt in it. Sometimes small insects and vermin take shelter within its bristles. If the broom is kept next to shoes or sandals, all this dust, as well as any insects, can get inside the footwear.

A person wears these shoes or sandals when he leaves the house. Should he leave in a hurry, he may not even think of examining his shoe. If there are insects nestled inside, or particles of dust have fallen in, then the footwear can be uncomfortable at best, and injurious in the worst case scenario. This belief originated from a health perspective, to avoid this situation.

Myths

5. We should not keep broken or old objects in the house.

Reality

When a person looks at the broken objects in his house a feeling of incompleteness can arise in him. Unattended old items which are covered with dust can induce a feeling of dullness and boredom.

When the broken objects are removed and the old objects cleaned, shining surfaces make the surrounding environment bright. If possible, one may replace old objects with sparkling, brightly-colored, new objects. Seeing these objects provides a soothing and pleasant feeling.

Any aspect of your life to which you pay attention consistently begins to impact your subconscious mind. The subconscious mind, then, relates the color and the shape of any object to thoughts and memories.

When a picture or an object is seen all the old memories associated with that object, which had been safely tucked away in the subconscious mind, come to the surface. Generally we don't have very good feelings associated with broken objects. Hence, looking at broken objects raises negative feelings. These feelings can have a very bad effect on the individuals looking at the objects. That's how that idea originally came into existence.

People who hold on to positive thoughts retain an optimistic outlook, even in seemingly negative situations. Such people are not affected by any external environment. On the contrary, their thoughts actually influence their surroundings. It's crucial, then, to first work on adjusting our outlooks. Until our outlooks are consistently positive, though, we can take advantage of this belief. We can keep our surroundings very clean, bright, and hygienic. In fact, there's no reason why we can't continue this good habit throughout our entire lives.

■ ■ ■

24
Superstitions related to Business

There are many myths, false beliefs, and superstitions surrounding business. In this chapter we'll explore some of them and give you an explanation for their development.

Myths

1. It is a bad omen if creditors visit a shop in the morning hours.

Generally, when a shopkeeper opens his shop in the morning he starts his day with the intention to have good business transactions ahead of him. The last thing he wants is to have money flow out of his pocket in the early hours. If a creditor walks into his store, then the shopkeeper is obligated to pay him the money which is due to him. You can see how a shopkeeper would consider that to be a bad beginning to the day. He may even internalize this feeling and believe that, on this day at least, he has failed in his duties. This may make him disappointed, and may even affect his attitude for the rest of the day. This, in turn, becomes reflected in all his transactions during the day. He may speak curtly with his customers. His anxious mind may cause him to commit blunders. By the end of the day, when he takes stock, he wrongly concludes that he had a very bad day. He puts the blame on the morning visit of the creditor. This leads to a sustained belief that visits by people who demand money in the morning hours is a bad omen for shopkeepers.

Revelation

Conversely, if a wealthy customer visits his shop in the morning and he strikes a good business deal, then the shopkeeper feels ecstatic. His positive state of mind lingers throughout the day, enabling him to accomplish much more than usual. He speaks politely with his customers. When he takes stock at the end of the day he feels very happy and satisfied with his accomplishments. He marks that day as one of the most successful and happy ones of his life.

In these examples we can easily see that the happiness and success of the shopkeeper solely depends on the external environment. He has, in effect, relinquished control of his fortune to the environment around him. Those who are able to control their thoughts do not fall prey to these types of situations. Regardless of any changes in the environment, and regardless of who walks through the door, they maintain their peaceful and happy state. Thus, nothing can be bad luck or a bad omen for them. Instead, they develop the ability to change every curse into a blessing.

Those who are trapped in blind beliefs turn blessings into curses. By focusing on unfavorable conditions they anticipate that something bad will happen. They not only anticipate it, but expect it. In effect, they create a self-fulfilling prophecy. When something bad does happen, they're able to rationalize and justify it, pointing to that particular incident as the catalyst. The fact of the matter is that their thoughts were the catalyst.

Myths

2. If you're a shopkeeper, don't read books while keeping shop. Also, don't sit with your arms crossed. These habits will make your business suffer.

Reality

This belief could have begun for several reasons:

a) *There's a possibility that* the shopkeeper would pay more attention to the *book than the administrative duties of the shop. He would start neglecting his business, and a number of things may go wrong. Just as a few examples, he might ignore his customers, calculate prices wrongly, or even not be aware enough to notice thefts in the shop.*

b) *The body language of a person with crossed arms gives the impression of someone with a closed mentality. A shopkeeper who looks unfriendly could potentially drive customers away. A person with open arms, though, invites openness in others. Body language that is open displays a willingness and readiness to serve.*

■ ■ ■

25
Superstitions related to Babies and Pregnant Women

L et's talk a bit now about some common misguided ideas concerning babies and pregnant women.

 **Myths**

1. Stepping over a baby brings the baby bad luck.

Stepping over a baby doesn't endow him with bad luck. It may, however, put the baby at physical risk.

Revelation

So how did this superstition originate?

a) Babies are soft and delicate. If someone steps over a baby, there is a possibility they may misstep and hit the baby with their foot. This may be dangerous for the baby. Babies have limited ways of verbalizing their pain. It's far too easy for the baby to even be trampled.

b) Apart from physical danger, a person's feet may carry germs and dirt which can be harmful for the baby.

c) While stepping over the baby the individual may drop something on him and injure him.

 Myths

2. Don't show a mirror to a baby.

Reality

The idea behind this myth has nothing to do with any calamitous event befalling either you or the baby.

A baby is unaware of his body. He can't recognize his face. He can see surrounding faces, but doesn't know that he has a face too. There is a possibility that the baby will become frightened when he sees his own face in the mirror.

 Myths

3.   Don't swing an empty cradle.

Reality

An empty cradle swings faster than one with a baby in it. When it swings without a baby occupying it, its joints and bolts become weak. This increases the chances of an accident occurring while the baby is in it.

 Myths

4.   Pregnant women should not use knives or sharp objects during a solar eclipse.

Reality

This belief developed with the baby's safety in mind. During a solar eclipse, magnetic waves in the environment may affect iron objects. These waves are harmful to the body. If a pregnant woman makes use of such objects, then it may prove to be harmful to the baby inside the womb. To avoid these waves iron articles should not be kept near the body. Pregnant women should avoid the use of such objects.

 **Myths**

5. A baby's hair should not be combed during the first year.

Reality

There was a good reason initially when this belief was developed. The sharp teeth of a comb can hurt the soft scalp of a baby.

 **Myths**

6. Shaving a baby's head is essential.

Reality

There was a good reason for this superstition.

a) *After you shave your head your hair grows longer and thicker. This ensures proper care of the hair.*

b) *Following the ceremony of shaving the head, blood flow to the scalp increases. Any dirt that was stuck to the scalp is cleaned off. Keeping the above two points in mind, it became a tradition to offer the baby's hair to God.*

 Myths

7. You should mark a baby with a black spot to protect him from the evil eye.

🔍 Reality

When people see beautiful things or a cute baby, many feel envious — especially when they don't have one themselves. It's not unusual, then, that beautiful things are given an ugly outward mark to avoid jealousy. Some people may choose to hang a black doll in the front of their beautiful house. This distracts people's attention from the beauty of the structure. Since it is human nature to point out faults, many individuals will pass by and only notice the unattractive doll, not the beauty of the house. A black spot, or a black thread tied around a baby's hand, diverts attention from his beauty as well. This belief was created to protect the child from the ill-will and jealousy of others.

■ ■ ■

26
Superstitions related to Animals

There are many superstitions surrounding animals, many of which have reasonable explanations. In this chapter, we'll examine a few of these.

 **Myths**

1. A lizard falling onto a person is a bad omen. One should take a bath immediately if a lizard falls on them.

 Reality

a) *A lizard is a creature that moves everywhere easily, whether it's in trees, on roofs, on walls, or just around on the ground. This means its feet are dirty. Besides this, a lizard's excretions contain acid. When it falls on someone it can indeed be harmful. For safety and health reasons, taking a bath is essential.*

b) *People with sensitive skin may have problems with the chemicals excreted by a lizard.*

c) *Lizards are poisonous. For the purpose of safety, edible items should not be kept open.*

 **Myths**

2. If a cat crosses your path, you'll have bad luck. Your work won't get done, or something ominous may occur.

 Reality

The genesis of this belief was to avoid road accidents. Cats, dogs, pigs, cows, goats, and rats are animals which often come in contact with humans. They used to be around in much larger numbers than they are today.

When a cat crosses a road quickly, it is probably for one of two reasons: either it's chasing some other animal, or it's being chased by some other animal. In any case, if someone tries to cross the cat's path, it increases the possibility of him getting attacked by those other animals. As a result, he may get injured. If he is travelling in a vehicle and suddenly stops to avoid hitting the animal, chaos may erupt, and other vehicles and pedestrians may be placed in danger.

To avoid these potentially dangerous events, the belief sprung up that you should slow down in these situations and wait for some time. This will prevent you from acting out of fear, and you will be able to face the situation calmly. When events settle down you can continue on.

This is the real reason for stopping when a cat crosses your path. Think about your safety, but don't let it become a superstition or an article of blind faith.

 Myths

3. The wailing or howling of a dog is a bad omen.

Reality

God created different creatures with different powers. An eagle can see the smallest creature on the ground while flying high, whereas an owl can see in the dark. The dog is an animal gifted with a powerful sense of smell. This amazing sense of smell is capable of detecting changes in the environment. Such changes may precede an impending earthquake, cyclone, or other disturbance which can affect humans.

A dog will howl or wail when it detects serious environmental disturbances. However, every time a dog wails isn't followed by a major natural disaster. Changes in the atmospheric condition occur quite often without any calamitous event happening. There is no need to fear the howls of dogs, or to spread rumors because of them.

You can send your opinion or feedback on this book to:
Tej Gyan Foundation, P.O. Box 25, Pimpri Colony,
Pimpri, Pune – 411017, Maharashtra, INDIA
Email: englishbooks@tejgyan.org

About Sirshree

(Symbol of Acceptance)

Sirshree's spiritual quest, which began during his childhood, led him on a journey through various schools of thought and prevalent meditation practices. His overpowering desire to attain the Truth made him relinquish his teaching profession. After a long period of contemplation on the truth of life, his spiritual quest culminated in the attainment of the ultimate truth. Since then, over the last two decades, he has dedicated his life toward elevating mass consciousness and making spiritual pursuit simple and accessible to all.

Sirshree espouses, "**All paths that lead to the truth begin differently, but culminate at the same point – understanding. Understanding is complete in itself. Listening to this understanding is enough to attain the truth.**"

Sirshree has delivered more than 3000 discourses that throw light on this understanding, simplify various aspects of life and unravel missing links in spirituality. He delivers the understanding in casual contemporary language by weaving profound aspects into analogies, parables and humor that provoke one to contemplate.

To make it possible for people from all walks of life to directly experience this understanding, Sirshree has designed the *Maha Aasmani Param Gyan Shivir* – a retreat designed as a comprehensive system for imparting wisdom. This system for wisdom, which has been accredited with ISO 9001:2015 certification, has inspired thousands of seekers from all walks of life to progress on their journey of the Truth. This system makes the wisdom accessible to every human being, regardless of religion, caste, social strata, country or belief system.

Sirshree is the founder of Tej Gyan Foundation, a no-profit organization committed to raising mass consciousness with branches in India, the United States, Europe and Asia-Pacific. Sirshree's retreats have transformed the lives of thousands and his teachings have inspired various social initiatives for raising global consciousness.

His published work includes more than 100 books, some of which have been translated in more than 10 languages and published by leading publishers. Sirshree's books provide profound and practical reading on existential subjects like emotional maturity, harmony in relationships, developing self-belief, overcoming stress and anxiety, and dealing with the question of life-beyond-death, to name a few. His literature on core spirituality expounds the deeper meaning of self-realization and self-stabilization, unravelling missing links in the understanding of karma, wisdom, devotion, meditation and consciousness.

Various luminaries and celebrities like His Holiness the Dalai Lama, publishers Mr. Reid Tracy, Ms. Tami Simon and Yoga Master Dr. B. K. S. Iyengar have released Sirshree's books and lauded his work. "The Source" book series, authored by Sirshree, has sold over 10 million copies in 5 years. His book, "The Warrior's Mirror", published by Penguin, was featured in the Limca Book of Records for being released on the same day in 11 languages.

Tejgyan... The Road Ahead
What is Tejgyan?

Tejgyan is the wisdom of the existential truth, which is beyond duality. "Gyan" is a term commonly used for "knowledge". Tejgyan is the wisdom beyond knowledge and ignorance. It is understanding that arises from direct experience of the final truth. It is what sets us free from the limitations of the mind and opens us to our highest potential.

In today's world, there are people who feel disharmony and are desperately trying to achieve balance in an unpredictable life. Tejgyan helps them in harmonizing with their true nature, the Self, thereby restoring balance in all aspects of their lives.

And then, there are those who are successful, but feel a sense of emptiness within. Tejgyan provides them fulfilment and helps them to embark on a journey towards self-realization. There are others who feel lost and are seeking the meaning of life. Tejgyan helps them to realize the true purpose of human life.

All this is possible with Tejgyan due to a very simple reason. The experience of the ultimate truth (God or Pure consciousness) is always available. The direct experience of this truth is possible provided the right method is known. Tejgyan is that method, that understanding.

The understanding of Tejgyan makes it possible to lead a life of freedom from fear, worry, anger and stress. It helps in attaining physical vitality, emotional strength and stability, harmony in relationships, financial freedom and spiritual progress.

At Tej Gyan Foundation, Sirshree imparts this understanding through a System for Wisdom – a series of retreats that guides participants step by step towards realizing the true Self, being established in the experience of self-realization, and expressing its qualities. This system for wisdom has been accredited with the ISO 9001:2015 certification.

Maha Aasmani Param Gyan Shivir

"**Maha Aasmani Param Gyan Shivir**" is the flagship Self-realization retreat offered by Tej Gyan Foundation. The retreat is conducted in Hindi. The teachings of the retreat are non-denominational (secular).

This residential retreat is held for 3 to 5 days at the foundation's MaNaN Ashram amidst the glory of the mountains and the pristine beauty of nature. The Ashram is located at the outskirts of the city of Pune in India, and is well connected by air, road and rail. The retreat is also held at other centres of Tej Gyan Foundation across the world.

You can participate in this retreat to attain ageless wisdom through a unique System for Wisdom so that you can:

1. Discover "Who am I" through direct experience.
2. Learn to abide in pure consciousness while functioning in the world, allowing the qualities of consciousness like peace, love, joy, compassion, abundance and creativity to manifest.
3. Acquire simple tools to use in everyday life, which help quiet the chattering mind.
4. Get practical techniques to be in the present and connect to the source of all answers within (the inner guru).
5. Discover missing links in the practices of Meditation (*Dhyana*), Action (*Karma*), Wisdom (*Gyana*) and Devotion (*Bhakti*).
6. Understand the nature of your body-mind mechanism to attain freedom form its tendencies.
7. Learn practical methods to shift from mind-centered living to consciousness-centered living.

A Mini-retreat is also conducted, especially for teenagers (14 to 16 years of age) during summer and winter vacations.

To register for retreats, visit www.tejgyan.org, contact (+91) 9921008060, or email mail@tejgyan.com

About Tej Gyan Foundation

Tej Gyan Foundation (TGF) was established with the mission of creating a highly evolved society through all-round development of every individual that transforms all the facets of their lives. It is a non-profit organization, founded on the teachings of Sirshree.

The Foundation has received the ISO certification (ISO 9001:2015) for its system of imparting wisdom. It has centres all across India as well as in other countries. The motto of Tej Gyan Foundation is 'Happy Thoughts'.

At the core of the philosophy of Tejgyan is the Power of Acceptance. Acceptance has profound meaning and is at the core of our Being. It is Acceptance that brings forth true love, joy and peace.

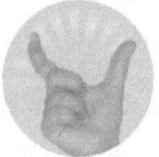

Symbol of Acceptance

The Symbol of Acceptance – shown above – is a representation of this truth. The symbol represents brackets. Whatever occurs in life falls within these brackets that signify acceptance of whatever is. Hence, this symbol forms the centerpiece of the Foundation's MaNaN Ashram.

The Foundation is creating a highly evolved society through:

- Tejgyan Programs (Retreats, YouTube Webcasts)
- Tejgyan Books and Apps
- Tejgyan Projects (Value education, Women empowerment, Peace initiatives)

The Foundation undertakes projects to elevate the level of consciousness among students, youth, women, senior citizens, teachers, doctors, leaders, professionals, corporate and Government organizations, police force, prisoners etc.

Now you can register online for the following retreats

Maha Aasmani Param Gyan Shivir
(5 Days Residential Retreat in Hindi)

Mini Maha Aasmani Shivir
3 Days (Residential) Retreat for Teens

🔍 www.tejgyan.org

Books can be delivered at your doorstep by registered post or courier. You can request the same through postal money order or pay by VPP. Please send the money order to either of the following two addresses:

WOW Publishings Pvt. Ltd.

1. Registered Office: E-4, Vaibhav Nagar, Near Tapovan Mandir, Pimpri, Pune - 411017.

2. Post Box No. 36, Pimpri Colony Post Office, Pimpri, Pune - 411017

Phone No: (+91) 9011013210 / 9623457873

You can also order your copy at the online store:
www.gethappythoughts.org

*Free Shipping plus 10% Discount on purchases above Rs. 500/-

For further details contact:
Tejgyan Global Foundation
Registered Office:

Happy Thoughts Building, Vikrant Complex, Near Tapovan Mandir, Pimpri, Pune 411017, Maharashtra, India.
Contact No: 020-27411240, 27412576
Email: mail@tejgyan.com

MaNaN Ashram:

Survey No. 43, Sanas Nagar, Nandoshi gaon, Kirkatwadi Phata, Sinhagad Road, Tal. Haveli, Dist. Pune 411024, Maharashtra, India.
Contact No: 992100 8060.

Hyderabad: 9885558100, **Bangalore:** 9880412588, **Delhi :** 9891059875, **Nashik:** 9326967980, **Mumbai:** 9373440985

For accessing our unique 'System for Wisdom' from self-help to self-realization, please follow us on:

	Website Online Shopping/ Blog	www.tejgyan.org www.gethappythoughts.org
	Video Channel	www.youtube.com/tejgyan For Q&A videos: http://goo.gl/YA81DQ
	Social networking	www.facebook.com/tejgyan
	Social networking	www.twitter.com/sirshree
	Internet Radio	http://www.tejgyan.org/internetradio.aspx

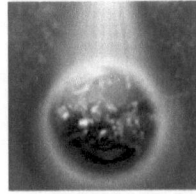

Pray for World Peace along with thousands of others every day at 09:09am and 09:09pm

Divine Light of Love, Bliss and Peace is Showering;
The Golden Light of Higher Consciousness is Rising;
All negativity on Earth is Dissolving;
Everyone is in Peace and Blissfully Shining;
O God, Gratitude for Everything!

www.ingramcontent.com/pod-product-compliance
Lightning Source LLC
LaVergne TN
LVHW040141080526
838202LV00042B/2983